D1357956

corrina wycoff's

fiction and essays have appeared in *Other Voices, New Letters, Coal City Review, The Oregon Quarterly, Brainchild, Out of Line, Golden Handcuffs,* and the anthologies: *Best Essays Northwest* and *The Clear Cut Future.* She holds an MFA in Creative Writing from the University of Oregon, and an MA in English from the University of Illinois, Chicago. She lives with her son in Seattle, Washington and teaches English and writing at Pierce College.

O STREET

STORIES

corrina wycoff

an imprint of
Other Voices
magazine

Chicago, Illinois

Copyright © 2006 by Corrina Wycoff

Portions of this book have appeared previously: "Afterbirth" in *New Letters* (Volume 65, no. 2), "The Shell Game" in *Coal City Review* (Volume 21), and "O Street" in *Other Voices* (Volume 45).

Library of Congress Cataloging-in-Publication Data

Wycoff, Corrina, 1971-
    O Street : stories / Corrina Wycoff.
        p. cm.
    ISBN 0-9767177-2-7
    1. Children of drug addicts--Fiction. 2. Mothers and daughters--Fiction.
    3. Poor--Fiction. I. Title.

    PS3623.Y35O19 2006
    813'.6--dc22

        2006033306

This collection is a work of fiction. Names, characters, places, and incidents are either the product of the author's imagination or are used fictitiously, and any resemblance to actual persons, living or dead, events, or locales is entirely coincidental.

Cover photo: Robin Hann
Author photo: Diane Grannis

Cover design by Melissa C. Lucar,
Fisheye Graphic Services, Inc., Chicago

Printed in the United States of America

10 9 8 7 6 5 4 3 2 1

Bookstores: OV Books titles are distributed by University of Illinois Press, phone (800) 621-2736 or www.press.uillinois.edu

www.othervoicesmagazine.org

CONTENTS

for Marcia Reinhard Waggoner

The Wrong Place
in the World

She didn't remember the address of St. Mary's Hospital. The cab driver, probably on purpose, took her to St. Mary's Church instead. Rather than pay a second fare, she decided to walk the remainder of the way, though the afternoon air was thick and humid and she sweat through the fabric of her shirt. Beth hadn't been back here, to Jersey City, since running away to Chicago on a Greyhound bus five years before, when she was seventeen. When she left, she had no plans to return. Ever. Then, early this morning, a stranger named Dr. George Brant telephoned to say that, yesterday, her mother had suffered congestive heart failure and was sure to die.

"You need to come to St. Mary's," Dr. George Brant had said. "Bring whatever money you can."

She'd run away on a summer Saturday, shortly after graduating high school. She told her mother she was going to work, left their apartment, and never came home. She didn't call her mother for months and, when she finally did, her mother only said, "I don't see that we have anything to talk about now," before asking her to send money. On Beth's birthdays and one or two other occasions each year since then, her mother had called from pay phones, asking for hundreds of dollars to be wired.

"Who was that?" Rachel, Beth's lover, asked after she'd hung up with Dr. Brant.

"My mother had a heart attack," she answered. She and Rachel had had a brutal quarrel the previous evening and, all night, it had hung thickly in the air, ruining her sleep. This new emergency seemed to dissipate it, and Beth felt strangely light.

Rachel said, "Go pack. I'll drive you to O'Hare."

She threw underwear, clothes, and pajamas into a carry-on bag. It reminded her of how she and her mother sometimes packed hastily in the early mornings, fleeing landlords or social workers or her mother's boyfriends. She wanted the memory to make her feel something, some kind of love for her mother, some kind of loss. But mostly, she felt proud to no longer know a life of head lice and evictions and Thanksgiving dinners at soup kitchens.

Rachel squeezed her hand. "You okay?"

"I don't know." Rachel's hand felt smooth and dry against her palm. "I don't want to go back there," she said, but Rachel led her to the car.

"It's your mom, Liz. You'll feel so sad if you don't get to say good-bye." Rachel let go of her hand and Beth shivered as if suddenly finding herself without clothes. The car smelled of air freshener and the cinnamon gum Rachel always chewed. Outside, the public transit train journeyed down a track on the freeway median.

At O'Hare Airport, Beth spent nine hundred dollars on a standby reservation, part of which would be refunded if her mother were to die and she could prove it. "Do you have enough money?" Rachel asked.

"Of course I do," Beth snapped.

On the plane to Newark, looking through the thick windowpane at a shaft of light poking through a hole in the clouds, Beth half expected her mother's ghost to float past, waving, smiling, on its way to whatever came next. A better place, Beth told herself, where she'll be better off. Instantly ashamed of her unkindness, she made herself imagine her mother's heart attack: the telltale pain in her mother's arm, her mother's strained phone call to 911 and collapse to the floor. She tried to imagine her mother's absolute isolation, how she probably fell without anyone nearby to catch or hold her or to wet her face with pretty tears. But these fantasies were scenes from movies and had nothing to do with Beth's mother. Her mother's isolation had always been impenetrable. She remembered chasing her mother down the tenement stairs many years earlier, calling, "Stop, Mom. Come home and go to bed." Her mother carried buckets of water that spilled with each step she took, making the gray cement stairs slick beneath Beth's sneakers.

It was two in the morning and, in the street, her mother washed strangers' cars and sang, "You're a Grand Old Flag" until the cops came. Now, Beth wandered those same streets, looking for St. Mary's Hospital. Many of the buildings had succumbed to utter decrepitude while others showed signs of gentrification, and although she could identify most of the buildings, the streetscape had altered enough to leave her unable to remember what any building was near. She walked, feeling dull-minded, as if stuck in a dream about being lost. On the streets that had not begun metamorphosing into condominium housing, the three-flats were connected to one another. If a bomb exploded in one house, the whole side of the street would topple. If one kitchen caught fire, the whole block would burn. This was the city in the old photographs Beth once, nervously, had shown Rachel. And Rachel had kissed her forehead and said, "Brave girl. You started a whole new life." That night, Beth cut the pictures into pieces too small to understand.

A whole new life, she now repeated to herself. Somewhere close, a fire hydrant had been opened. She heard children's relieved squeals and recognized the peculiar smell of fresh water sizzling against asphalt. She remembered running tiptoe across unbearably hot streets to plunge her burning soles in rapidly growing, warming, dirtying puddles being made by the hydrant. She remembered Pepino, the Sicilian barber, who could always be persuaded to open the hydrant in front of his shop and the rust-corroded wrench he used to let the water out. "Ole!" he'd say, absurdly, as he watched the children splash. She remembered the airy pitch of his voice. Then she remembered that St. Mary's Hospital stood right outside Hamilton Park, and precisely how to get there from where she stood. As she walked, she half expected that every local seated on these ragged stoops would recognize her instantly and shout, "Beth Dinard! You haven't changed a bit!"

But I have changed, she reminded herself. *Anyone looking at me would think that I'm a tourist lost on the way to the Statue of Liberty ferry.* She imagined standing over her mother's hospital bed. Her mother would gaze up at her, seeing a smooth-haired twenty-two-year-old woman in an understated blouse and smart eye-glasses, and she would barely be able to remember the skinny, long-ago girl everyone called Beth—a girl with ratted bangs, black eyeliner, mutilated ears, and a harsh and nasal accent. "I'm sorry I didn't tell you I was going," Beth would say. "But I'm not sorry that I went."

"You got out," her mother would answer, proudly. Then she'd die, and this part of Beth's life would die too.

An enormous statue of the Madonna occupied the hospital lobby, its great head lowered, its eyes fixed in an expression of vacant serenity. Beth asked the receptionist for her mother's room number and learned that her mother was not a patient in the Cardiac Care Unit or any other unit. She learned that George Brant was not a physician at St. Mary's, or maybe anywhere. "You might want to try City General?" the receptionist offered, not kindly, before turning away to answer a ringing telephone. Beth thanked the receptionist in a voice that sounded as if someone far away was talking. Mary's inscrutable stone face stared down from above her and, below her, the floor seemed to move, as though it had transformed into a conveyor belt.

She needed air, walked a few blocks to Pavonia Avenue and sat on the curb. She and her mother had lived on Pavonia when Beth was ten or eleven years old. It was around that time, she remembered now, that her mother pretended to have been diagnosed with "inoperable floating tumors" that allegedly left her only six months to live. "What will you do," she had sobbed, "when I'm gone?" In tears at school, Beth had confided in her teacher who'd angrily said, "There's no such thing as a floating tumor, Beth," as if Beth were the liar.

Her mother hadn't called asking for money in probably six months. Now Beth wished that, during that last conversation, she had asked her mother for more information than the most convenient Western Union outpost. She didn't know her mother's address or telephone number. She wished she could go to her mother's apartment and yell, "Aren't you supposed to be dead?"

Her mother must have asked a friend to pose as a doctor, call Beth, and get her to fly east on a second's notice as a perverse prank. The alleged Dr. Brant had said to bring money. Maybe her mother wanted more than Beth could send over a wire. If so, she had to be someplace nearby, trailing her, waiting. But why now?

"Are you new?"

One of the neighborhood girls stood in front of her. It was weird to see one of them by herself—when Beth was a kid she roamed in a pack. The unwashed red-brown hair around the child's ears was matted, and there were knee-holes in her brown corduroys. She looked to be about eight years old. A key dangled from a piece of yarn around her neck. "New at what?"

The girl didn't answer. She pointed to one of the row houses across the street and said, "Do you see Mrs. Palma up there on the third floor? She just had a baby."

Beth didn't see anyone in the curtainless window. "Where?"

"She's prob'ly feeding him. She don't go in front of the window when she's feeding him 'cause her booby's out."

"Where's your mother?" Beth asked. She adjusted her wristwatch to Eastern Time. It was quarter past four.

The girl shrugged. "I'm watching for her. Where's *your* mother?"

Beth said, "She's dead."

The girl sat down on the curb. "I'm April. What school do you go to?"

"I'm a grown-up, April. I'm done with school. I work for a company now and make money."

"Forget it, then." The girl stood, shoved her hands into her front pockets, and walked down the street without looking back. Forget what? Again, she glanced at Mrs. Palma's window. Now she saw the long-haired woman, the baby over one of her shoulders with its back toward the street. Because the window had no screens, there wasn't much keeping this woman and her baby on the safe side of it, and Beth half expected her to toss the baby out onto the sidewalk. She wondered if she could run across the street quickly enough to catch it.

Her mother wasn't listed in the phone book or information. She wasn't a patient at Christ Hospital or City General. So Beth walked street after street, muttering, "This is the very last time you'll humiliate me," until her footsteps seemed to join in and say, "last time, last time, last time." When evening came, she walked around St. Mary's again—it was the place she'd been summoned to, after all—but her mother wasn't there. April was still outside, though, writing on the side of an electrical box with a piece of chalk. When the girl waved, Beth thought she saw her mother's face replicated in April's.

"What's your mother's name, April?"

"I'm not hurting the box that bad. I'm not writing the F-word on it or nothing."

"What's her name anyhow? I'm not going to tattle."

"Her name's Mom, stupid."

"What's your last name, then?"

"McGovern."

The name was wrong, but, to Beth, the resemblance was suddenly unmistakable. "Is that your mom's last name too?"

"How should I know?" April's eyebrows pressed together as Beth moved closer to her. Her body was like a squirrel's, alert and twitching toward escape. "You work for the school or something?"

Beth moved even closer and knelt down to the girl's eye level. "No."

April took a step backward. "Then what do you care?"

"Just curious." She made her voice as gentle as she could, but the girl continued to back away. Her pupils dilated and her lips grew pale.

"Curiosity killed the cat," April yelled. She picked up half a broken bottle from the ground, hurled it at Beth, and ran.

Beth's forehead stung where the glass had hit it. This girl had to belong to her mother, she decided. She was milling around St. Mary's Hospital, and she seemed to have her mother's smile. Her last name didn't match, but so what? The kid probably lied. Beth herself had lied with alacrity when she was April's age. She approached the electrical box. In jagged letters, the girl's graffiti message read, "My white cat sitting in my window fills the whole window. Looks painted on." Beth decided to secure a hotel room and return.

She flagged a cab. "Take me to a hotel that isn't too terrible," she commanded. The driver grinned and drove to the York Motel, a dingy two-story box situated close to the railroad tracks, where Route 9 became a street with a name. "This is about what you meant, wasn't it?" the driver asked.

"No," she answered. "Does this look like what I meant?"

"I wouldn't know. Twenty-three fifty for the fare."

"That can't be right."

"Twenty-three fifty," he repeated, and turned on his not-for-hire light.

Beth looked for another cab, but it wasn't the kind of neighborhood they came to. Down the street, a group of teenage boys played dominoes, slamming down tiles and calling out numbers. "Four's the spinner," one of them yelled. They seemed to look at her with casual menace. She ran into the dirty hotel lobby.

"I need to use your phone," she told the old man behind the desk. He had a swollen, puckered nose and bloodshot eyes.

"There are phones in the rooms."

"I need to call a cab," she explained. "I want to be taken to a different hotel."

"There are phones in the rooms," he repeated. "Sixty dollars a night. Forty-five for you."

"I'm not staying here."

"Suit yourself." He committed his attention to a television mounted on the wall. Static distorted the picture, blurring actors into suggestions of people.

Beth had to find the girl and her mother before dark. "Fine," she said, slamming forty-five dollars onto the front desk. "I haven't got time."

"Suit yourself," the man said again, handing her a clipboard. "Sign at the bottom for your linens."

The "linens" consisted only of a yellowish top sheet and an unevenly stained fitted sheet with stretched-out elastic. Her dark room smelled of bleach and the bed could vibrate for a quarter. The walls were bare except for a small cartoon hanging in the bathroom that pictured a little girl seated on an oversized toilet above the caption, "But I AM trying!" Beth tried to lift the frame from the wall and discovered it was attached with cement.

After calling for a cab, she thought of telephoning Rachel, but Rachel's presence felt utterly at odds with this grimy hotel room and the insanity of Beth's not-dead mother. Rachel was raised cleanly, and her life had been a series of clean successes. At twenty-seven, she'd finished a doctorate in English and had gotten an assistant professorship. Three years afterward, she was granted tenure quickly without ever having to change schools. Beth met Rachel a year before, at a bar near the university where Rachel taught, when Rachel had just turned thirty-two and Beth had just turned twenty-one. Rachel was only Beth's second lover. The first was a much older woman named Gina, from whose thrall Rachel had saved Beth. Rachel, on the other hand, had had a succession of intellectual, well-to-do lovers, both men and women. Rachel's men fascinated and appalled Beth. She liked to think about them for the jolt of pain it caused, just as she once had enjoyed touching the electric guard fence around the lions at the zoo. "It's not that I think I'm straight," Rachel once told her, "I'm just saying that sexuality isn't rigid. Especially in academia." Beth hated the way Rachel always lingered over the syllables in "academia" as if it were a kind of expensive body lotion.

It wasn't that Beth was stupid. She just wasn't smart in the ways Rachel probably valued. She could learn just about any office system in record time, for example, even when no one taught her how. It was this ability combined with her impeccable attendance that had earned her a promotion to administrative assistant from her first office job as a receptionist and then, recently, had earned her a second promotion to office manager, a job that paid her a salary rather than an hourly wage, enabled her to have a small savings account and, most importantly, let her solve the one problem she'd most wanted to: how to make it, however tenuously, out of the underclass. Sometimes Rachel criticized Beth's preoccupation with money in the manner of someone, Beth believed, who'd never had to worry about it. Rachel knew better, of course, than to outwardly mock

Beth for having been poor. But Beth believed that was exactly what Rachel was doing whenever she said, "I just don't understand why you think class has to do with money and not education." Now, sitting on the York Hotel bed, Beth realized that her money had not protected her, and wondered if Rachel's education would have. Rachel, it seemed, could never have landed in circumstances like these. Beth decided to wait until after she found April again before calling Rachel. Then she would call and say, "Guess what, honey? My mother left us an orphan to raise."

The child wasn't stationed anywhere near Saint Mary's, so Beth waited on Pavonia Avenue, on the stoop across from the spot where she first saw her. One nearby building looked the most disheveled; its façade was freckled with black tar patches and hasty graffiti—gang shout-outs and careless insults. In the window next to the building's front door, a white cat sat perfectly still.

"APRIL!" She hoped the little girl or her own mother would appear. She imagined taking April's face in her hands. Their mother, if lucid, would say, "Go on, make something out of her. Give her the kind of life I never could." If she wasn't lucid, she probably wouldn't say anything to Beth or April, not even good-bye; instead she'd stand there quoting, "The Wasteland" or asking, "Do you know what happened to Amy Carter?" as if Beth and April were strangers.

"APRIL!" Beth called again.

From the windows above her came a cacophony of insults shouted in English, Spanish, and Sicilian that Beth was unable to out-shout. About a block down the sidewalk, three girls jumped rope to "Miss Lucy" in the dusk-light, and Beth ran to them.

"You guys know April McGovern?"

The girls looked at each other as if Beth were a panhandler. "You're up, Anna," the biggest of the three girls said to one of the others as she took the ends of the vinyl clotheslines they used as jump ropes. She nodded to the other rope turner and the ropes started spinning. Anna stood with her elbows bent, wincing as she watched the ropes turn. "Come *on!*" the big girl yelled. "Jump in, already!" Did they really think they could just ignore her? Beth moved closer to them, waiting.

"You're doing it too fast!" Anna whined, glancing back at Beth who stood close enough now to feel the whistling breeze the ropes made.

"Don't be such a baby," the other rope turner said, but she looked at Beth too, and her voice sounded small and nervous.

"Can I jump in?" Beth asked.

The big girl looked at Anna as if she'd decided that Beth was a harmless lunatic, and nodded her head to the left. Anna said, "Go ahead," in a tentative voice and sprinted out of Beth's way.

"Come on," the big girl said. "Let's slow it down for the old lady."

Beth watched the ropes turn, felt their rhythm in her body as she had when she was a child, and jumped in. She made it through half of "Miss Lucy" before she lost sight of the ropes and the girls. Now she only saw Rachel, as Rachel might look giving a talk at an upcoming conference. One of Rachel's former lovers—who taught at Wellesley and with whom Rachel had once been "smitten"—would be there. Beth imagined Rachel saying words like "epistemology" while the Wellesley man, in a crisp gray suit, sat in the audience clapping and clapping. One of the ropes caught around her ankle.

"You spin now," Anna said, inching her way slowly back to the group, not daring, it seemed, to get too close to Beth. "I'm up."

The big girl handed Beth the ropes, maybe too careful to not let her hands touch Beth's. Beth grabbed the ropes, let her thumb brush against the big girl's wrist, and watched the girl pull away quickly before meeting Beth's gaze with a naked, frightened look. She wanted to tell the girl that it was okay, that she was April's sister, that she had jumped rope in this very spot when she was little. But saying any of that might have undone everything she'd become. Instead, she stared into the big girl's eyes until the girl looked away. Then she spun the ropes. Fast.

"I *can't!*" Anna whined.

Beth slowed the ropes and Anna stood blinking.

"I'll go." The big girl pushed Anna out of the way and jumped in. She did things Beth had never been brave enough to try as a child. She squatted on all fours and performed quarter turns between jumps.

She hopped from one foot to two feet, snapped up onto her hands and back down again.

"You're good!" Beth told the girl, surprised by the humility in her voice. Then she looked at the other rope turner and asked, "Can you do that fancy stuff too?"

"Nah," the girl answered; then she pointed to Anna and said, "But I'm better'n *her*. She never even jumps in."

"I do too," Anna whined, "with my other friends."

When the big girl finished, she glared at Beth as if her skill would protect her, and Beth felt sorry for her, because she hadn't found the protection she thought she had. In five years, all her fancy tricks wouldn't mean anything; they'd just be part of a game she'd remember playing. "You could do TV commercials, you know," Beth told her. "Make enough money to start a whole new life."

"That's what my mom says," the girl sighed, "but she took me to this lady in New York that's supposed to help and the lady said I'm too fat."

"An agent?"

"No. She was called something else."

"Manager." Anna looked at Beth and rolled her eyes. "I'm her sister. I heard the whole story five million times."

"So." Beth decided to try again. "You guys know April McGovern?"

The girls looked at each other and their apprehension seemed to come back. "Yeah," the chubby girl finally answered. "We know Bink. What'd she do?"

"Nothing. I'm just looking for her. You know her mother?"

"Ms. McGovern?" The girls smiled at each other. "Yeah, we know her."

"What's wrong with her? Is she crazy or something?"

"Crazy," Anna answered, still smiling. She looked at the big girl, who winked.

"Is she old?"

"She's pretty old, like maybe even older than you."

"You know where I can find her?"

"Ms. McGovern?" the chubby girl said. "Good luck! She lives over there." She pointed down the street.

"In the house with the cat in the window?"

"Yeah. Malcom. That's Bink's cat."

"Do you know where I could find April?"

"She's around here somewhere," Anna offered. "You could leave her a note. C'mon. It's my turn. Are we jumping or not?"

The ropes spun again for Anna to watch apprehensively. A note. Beth walked to the five-and-dime, bought a pack of unlined index cards, tape, and a felt-tip pen. She felt hungry now and walked several blocks to Lombardi's 24-Hour Eats where, long ago, she and her mother used to splurge on dollar omelets called Hobos. Over a plate of eggs, she'd figure out the best way to phrase her rescue offer to April.

Her waitress was at least six feet tall, pale, skinny, and topped with short hair curly enough to look itchy. A large pimple shone in the center of her forehead. Beth stirred sugar into her coffee and opened the menu. It was a full color affair with photographs of beehive-blond waitresses wearing pink dresses and red lipstick. Their thin, pink arms, elbows cocked, ended in white plates topped with cheeseburgers. Long ago, she might have wished to have her own picture on a menu, or that *she* was jump-roping in TV commercials, so that her mother could point to her image and brag, "She's mine. Would you look at that?" But now the photographed women made her sad, and she imagined Rachel (if Rachel, by some horrible accident wound up eating in a place like this) saying, "This menu would be a fun semiotics exercise for my students."

"Refill?" the oily-browed giraffe of a waitress asked, coffee pot tilted over Beth's half-empty cup.

Beth nodded and the giraffe walked away without further conversation. She opened the pack of index cards, removed one and wrote:

Your white cat
Sitting in your window
Fills the whole window
Looks painted on.

"What's that? Haiku?" the giraffe asked, placing Beth's plate on the table.

"I think haiku have three lines, don't they?"

"There's more than one kind of haiku, you know."

"I know," Beth said.

"You want ketchup for your eggs?"

Beth nodded. The giraffe pulled a plastic ketchup bottle from her apron pocket and, as if decorating a cake, meticulously drew the outline of a cat on Beth's eggs. Before walking away, she lowered her face level with Beth's and gruffly said, "Meow."

Beth crumpled up the maybe-haiku, took out a second index card and wrote, "April, what kind of food do you like to eat? I will cook for you and keep you happy. Your white cat Malcom can come too."

Where should she tell the girl to meet her? She hadn't planned on going back to the York Motel. But she couldn't possibly ask her to come to Lombardi's where several hanging signs read THIRTY MINUTE LIMIT FOR CONSUMING FOOD in an attempt to prevent loitering. She considered waiting outside somewhere but remembered the nights she spent outside as a child, the dark hours passing slowly, dangerously, while she tried to nap on the library steps or behind the convenience store, between the garbage dumpsters. She had no choice. She wrote, "I am at the York Motel. Room 232 on the second floor. Your sister, Beth."

"All set?" A waitress who was not the giraffe placed a check on her table.

"Where'd the other lady go?"

The new waitress raised an eyebrow. "Lunch."

Beth paid the bill and left the diner. When she didn't see the girl on Pavonia, she taped the index card to the outside windowsill. The white cat clawed and hissed at her through the screen.

From across the street, the card was barely visible. So Beth took another from the pack and wrote, "You can tell a lot about people by the way they treat their pets." Then, on a third, "Come with me into a new life." She sat on the curb writing messages on index cards until her butt ached and night had come. Finally, the taped cards covered the windowsill, the tar patches below it, and the upper half of the window itself.

She'd forgotten this city's night sounds. Now, in her motel room, she reflexively imagined gunshots at the sound of every backfiring bus. The door had no deadbolt or chain, only a doorknob lock that could probably be broken easily. She wanted to block her front door, but all the furniture in the room was bolted to the floor. A radio played in the room next door. Beth wished the motel trusted its tenants with TVs.

April would certainly have gotten the notes by now. She had probably even shown the display to her mother. It was after ten at night. Why didn't anyone come?

She needed another plan. Tomorrow, she decided, she would find those girls again and wait with them for April to come around. Tomorrow night, she and April would be on a plane home. And if April got scared or homesick, Rachel would tell April the same thing she told Beth whenever Beth worried aloud that she would abruptly lose her job and wind up homeless. "Be reasonable," Rachel always said. "There is such a thing as before and after."

The radio music next door stopped and now heavy footsteps sounded, marching up and down the wooden outdoor motel stairs. Then something scratched at her front door. The door had no peephole and the window didn't give Beth an adequate view.

"April?" she called tentatively. "Hello?"

"Hello?" a man's voice next door mimicked through the wall. "Hello!"

The scratching grew louder. "Who's there?" she shouted.

"Who's there?" mocked the man next door.

"I mean it. Tell me who's out there!"

"I mean it," the parrot laughed.

She banged on the wall. "Will you shut up?"

"You shut up!" a different man's voice yelled back. "No one's calling for your ugly ass."

She slumped against the wall. Her neighbor was right. The scratching didn't come from her front door, but from behind the baseboards. Through a gap in the plaster in the far corner of the room, Beth thought she saw the naked pink tip of a rat's tail poking through. She put her wallet in her back pocket and bolted to the office.

"Leaving?" asked the man at the lobby desk.

"You have rats." Beth slid her room key across the desk and ran. She heard the man call out, "What about the linens?"

She ran fast among the headlights and streetlights. Sirens blared from every direction and car alarms whooped. The night air was hot and stagnant and each of her breaths felt heavy and wet.

She ran to Pavonia Avenue, found April's house, and noted that the messages she'd left still hung on the window. A woman who was not Beth's mother stood on the front stoop. She looked out into the street awhile then returned to the house where she appeared beside April's cat Malcom in the lit living room window. Then the light clicked off.

Beth's lungs felt waterlogged from running in the humid heat. April was not her sister, her mother wasn't dying or anywhere to be found, and there seemed to be no reason for this trip. The muscle knot under her right shoulder blade throbbed, and she wished Rachel was with her. Sometimes, after Rachel and Beth fought, after Beth brought up the Wellesley man and said, "You don't love me the way you loved him," Rachel lowered her head in a pose Beth considered too submissive for her breeding and asked, "Do you want a back rub?" And even though Rachel's touch couldn't entirely erase her worry, it sometimes dulled it just enough, especially when Rachel said soothing, patronizing things like, "You poor girl. Poor diaspora girl." Beth had never heard the words "diaspora" or "embourgeoisement" until she met Rachel. The words she herself had used were "homesick" and "The Man."

The offer of backrubs might not have been enough for her in Chicago, but in this world that gesture felt like more love than she would ever deserve. She walked slowly now, enervated by disappointment. The street stood empty. A car waited briefly at the corner stop sign and turned.

"So you're back." The giraffe stood at her table, order book in hand. Beth didn't know why she answered, "I'm waiting for my mother."

"You want a cuppa joe or something while you're waiting?"

"I'll have a corn muffin too. Toasted."

The corn muffin arrived and she ate it slowly. In the booth next to hers, two young women sat silently eating omelets. They wore hospital orderly uniforms and their eyes looked drowsy. Beth thought, *That would have been my fate if I'd stayed here, graveyard shifts and rounded shoulders.* One of the girls blocked her mouth from Beth's view, said something to her coworker. Then they glanced at Beth, looked back to each other, and giggled. *You recognize me, don't you?* Beth wanted to say. *You think I haven't changed, but I have.*

She must have said some of that aloud, because one of the orderlies replied, "Good for you." Then she lowered her head and giggled again.

After eating, she stood outside the diner, trying to figure out where to go next. Eventually she'd have to run across her mother. Eventually, her mother would have to turn up and tell her why she'd summoned her. The night grew later and even the river drafts didn't break the air's hot stillness. Briefly, she wondered what would happen if she made her way out to the suburbs—only an hour or so from here, but a whole different realm all the same—where Rachel grew up. When Rachel first told her that, Beth must have looked at her derisively, because in a bristly, defensive voice, Rachel had said, "It's not the wrong place in the world to be from, you know. You just have a chip on your shoulder."

The Wellesley man hailed from Rachel's suburb too. The night before Dr. Brant's phone call, Rachel had told her how she and the Wellesley man, "always rode horses together" over the holidays.

"Will you do that this year too?" Beth asked, a cold, black panic cutting her breathing short. They were sitting together on the couch, having just finished watching an old French film Rachel had rented from an expensive, arts-only video store that checked prospective customers' credit ratings before granting them borrowing privileges.

"Sure," Rachel said, "but it's nothing to worry about."

"Why would I worry?" Beth mocked, standing, moving away from Rachel. "It's not like you were ever *smitten* with him or anything."

"It's not like that anymore," Rachel answered. Then, "You know, he'll be out here for a conference in a couple of weeks. You can meet each other."

"Why do you want us to meet?" she snapped. "So you can show off how much you're slumming?"

Rachel stayed seated on the couch, looking down so Beth couldn't see her expression. "I don't think of us that way," she said.

"Are you laughing?" Beth wasn't sure.

"Right." Rachel sounded frustrated. "I'm always making fun of you. I think you're the lowest of the low. Rock bottom."

"You shouldn't even be able to say something like that."

"This is impossible," Rachel said, her eyes half-closed. When Rachel looked exhausted and defeated, Beth thought she seemed also at her most human, her most capable of giving love.

Now Beth wondered what would happen if, instead of meeting her own mother on this trip, she met Rachel's. If she could somehow charm Rachel's mother, get her mother to accept her, invite her in, then maybe Rachel wouldn't reconcile with the Wellesley man at the conference or when they rode horses. But Rachel's mother didn't know about Beth; she didn't even know that Rachel dated women. Rachel had once said, "I think the reason I kept trying with men was to make her happy."

"Even the Wellesley man?" Beth had asked hopefully. "Your mother must have loved him."

"She did. But I did too. There was really something there with him."

I should just go back to the airport, Beth finally decided, and she stood at the curb hoping for a taxi. She only saw headlights of ordinary cars and dark outlines of jaywalkers. She wanted Rachel. She wanted to take her mother's shoulders in her hands and shake them until her skeleton broke apart.

"You're still here?"

Beth didn't recognize the voice but turned, half expecting to see her mother. Instead, the giraffe stood behind her, a striped macramé purse looped over one wrist.

"I thought my mother might come."

"At this hour?"

"No. I mean, I'm giving up. Now I'm just waiting for a cab to take me back to the airport."

"A cab? At this hour?"

Beth expected the giraffe to leave, but she didn't. She had to crane her neck excessively in order to look into her eyes.

"I don't have a car," the giraffe said, "or I'd take you there myself. What time's your flight?"

"I haven't booked it yet."

"I see."

They stood staring silently until Beth's neck throbbed and she lowered her head to face the woman's square shoulders and narrow chest. Then she collapsed her head onto her stomach, wrapped her arms around her rib cage, and cried.

Beth felt a large hand atop her head, and the giraffe's purse swinging rhythmically into the back of her neck.

"It's okay," the giraffe said. "Hey there, it's okay."

"I have nowhere to go," Beth sobbed. "The York Motel has rats and my mother was supposed to be dead."

"Hey," the giraffe continued. "It's okay. I'll take you home with me."

Beth did not disengage her arms from their place around the giraffe as they began walking. She kept her head buried in her coat and let herself be led. She didn't know how many blocks they walked, but could feel the giraffe turning corner after corner. A passerby laughed, "That girl's wasted." The giraffe's thin, scratchy windbreaker—or maybe the woman herself—smelled of cooking grease and sweat.

"Okay, we're here." The giraffe didn't pronounce Rs at the ends of words.

Beth lifted her face and blinked herself back into single vision. The giraffe's three-flat looked like many others in town: crumbling brownstone, cracked concrete steps with large holes indicating where railings once were. The windows on either side of the steps were barred and one of the panes behind the bars was cracked. A string of garlic dangled over the front entrance.

"We go down," the giraffe said, walking ahead of her down a second smaller stairwell that led to the basement apartment. A rickety black mailbox hung on the door. She opened the mailbox and pawed through its contents but didn't remove whatever she found before unlocking the totem of deadbolts and ducking through the entranceway to avoid hitting her head on the doorframe.

"Hey boy!" she called out in a pet-greeting voice as she turned on the overhead light. An undersized stegosaurus occupied a cage in the middle of the mottled linoleum floor.

"Jesus Christ!"

"What's the matter with you?" the giraffe laughed. "You never saw an iguana before?" She opened the cage, lifted the lizard and cuddled it to her chest. Its head was level with hers and its tail reached all the way down to her knees. "You want your chicken, don't you?" she asked the creature as she procured a small plastic bag filled with bits of cooked meat from her purse. She tenderly held chunks of the colorless stuff up to the iguana's mouth. The iguana ate placidly for several minutes then squirmed toward the floor.

"He gets ravenous when I work these double shifts, poor thing. Make yourself at home, hon."

The stifling apartment consisted of one cramped room. Beth felt a sharp hunger pang for her own nine-hundred-dollar-a-month studio apartment in a Lincoln Park high-rise. Lincoln Park was north of downtown Chicago, but several miles south and east of the poorer northside neighborhoods, and her apartment featured new appliances, an island kitchen, and a view of the boats docked in Diversey Harbor. Here, an old, stained counter, stove, refrigerator, and sink lined the back wall. There were several large pillows to Beth's right and a mattress covered with sleeping bags and a green and burgundy comforter on the floor to her left. The open bathroom door revealed that the shower curtain matched the comforter. A telephone topped an overturned empty milk crate and, again, Beth felt a reflexive need for Rachel.

She put the side of her finger into her mouth and bit down hard until the feeling passed.

The giraffe disappeared into the bathroom and the iguana found his way back into his cage; he stared at the open cage door as if he wished he could obtain some privacy.

"Your lizard looks a little put out that I'm here," Beth called toward the bathroom door.

"I couldn't hear ya, hon." The giraffe reemerged in a long, pink bathrobe. "I had the water running." Then she locked the iguana's cage and said, "Don't mind him. He's an old sweetie." Beth didn't move from her place on the cushion. A WNBA poster hung on the wall above the giraffe's bed. There was no closet but several pants and skirts hung from plastic hangers on a metal clothes rack. Beneath the rack sat a half-filled laundry basket and a small heap of obscenely large shoes.

The woman sat across the room from Beth with her feet resting against the side of the iguana's cage. "I'm ex-*hau*-sted," she said. "Let's say we hit the hay."

Beth had expected the giraffe to ask questions or at least intimate some degree of curiosity. She wondered whether inviting strangers to sleep in her apartment was something she did routinely.

"Lemme get you some PJs and blankets." The giraffe stood, took the comforter and one sleeping bag off the mattress and a T-shirt from the clothes rack. "Here," she said, handing the shirt to Beth, "I'd offer you pajama pants but I know they'd never fit."

"That's okay. I've got…" Beth realized she no longer had her carry-on bag. "Oh no!"

"What's a matter?"

"I lost my luggage!"

"You didn't leave it at Lombardi's did you? I got keys to there. We could go back."

"I don't know." She tried to remember whether she'd brought her bag to the diner. No, she'd been empty-handed there. Both times. And in the store. And at St. Mary's Hospital. "I left it in the taxi I took from the airport this morning."

"Tough luck. You'll never get it back. Here, you go get changed and I'll make up your bed."

The giraffe's bathroom had clean, white tiles on the floor and walls, and an unlabeled prescription bottle stood on the sink with its cap off. The large yellow pills were unmarked and Beth considered taking one just to see what it might do. The borrowed T-shirt read BASKETBALL IS LIFE, and hung past Beth's knees. She wondered if the woman had played. Maybe she'd even been a college star with a fat scholarship. Maybe she'd gotten badly injured in her rookie season, lost everything, and now took pills to quell the residual pain. Tough luck, she had said about Beth's bag, you'll never get it back. *Maybe it's a good way of looking at things*, Beth thought. It had instantly cauterized any panic she might have felt about her luggage. She tried to imagine how much easier her life might be if she could make herself say, "Tough luck, I'll never get her back," whenever she imagined losing Rachel. But she knew that, without Rachel, she wouldn't exist even half as much.

The giraffe had spread the sleeping bag and comforter on the floor beside the cushions and was in her own bed on the other side of the room when Beth came out of the bathroom.

"Couldya hit the lights, hon? Once I'm down, I'm down for the count."

"Sure," Beth agreed. She flicked off the lights, groped her way to the makeshift bed, and nestled beneath a thin sheet. *Down for the count*, she repeated silently. On the other hand, maybe the giraffe subsisted on hopelessness. *Maybe*, she thought, *hope is what makes me hold on to Rachel. Maybe if I hold on long enough, I'll grow into someone new— someone who could easily have had two parents, good breeding, hearty suppers and piano lessons. But if I lose hope and let go, Rachel will leave, and I'll have nothing.* The streetlights eked through the apartment's single, high window. Shadows of the window bars spanned the floor. Beth wondered whether iguanas slept with their eyes closed.

"You comfy over there?" the giraffe's voice sounded.

"Fine. Yeah. Thanks."

Chair legs scraped the floor above Beth's head and she heard a woman laugh. She wanted to nuzzle against Rachel's smooth neck, to wrap her arm around her thin waist until Rachel pushed it away, gently saying, "Okay now. Too much." She wished the giraffe were a different kind of stranger, a sage who'd hear her story in full and tell her how she could rid herself of this city forever, how she could become the kind of person Rachel would never want to leave. "Hey," Beth whispered, "what's your name anyhow?"

"Rita," the giraffe answered.

"I'm Liz. Dinard."

"Well, don't be a chatterbox, Liz Dinard," Rita sighed. "I'm tired."

Beth's lungs and eyes burned as if she'd been crying all day. She turned her back toward the iguana cage, closed her eyes, and was relieved to feel herself on the verge of sleep.

It was still dark when she woke to the banging, moaning sound of old water pipes. Someone upstairs must have been showering. It was a sound Beth had forgotten and, for probably a full minute after it woke her, she was disoriented enough to half-suspect herself back in a childhood apartment she'd shared with her mother. Then she rolled over, saw the streetlight glittering faintly on the iguana cage and remembered where she was and how she'd gotten there.

"Rita?" she whispered, but no response came. So Rita must've lived in this apartment for a while; she'd evidently become fully habituated to the noise. In the dream she'd had before waking, she'd been lying beside Rachel's breasts, but when she'd reached for her lover's body, her hands had hit hard against a force field that protected Rachel from Beth's touch. "You shouldn't have gone home," the dream-Rachel said in Rita's voice. "You look different when you're there." *No*, Beth pleaded silently now, trying to make her thoughts reach across the country to where Rachel lay. *No, please. I don't want to belong here. I want to belong with you.*

She groped to the giraffe's phone; the cord was long enough to reach the bathroom. She closed the door and dialed the number in the dark. It rang twelve times before a man's voice grumbled, "Yeah?"

"I've got the wrong number," Beth stammered. "I'm sorry."

"You should be," the man barked. "You have any idea what time it is?"

Beth hung up the phone. Had she just heard the voice of the Wellesley man, in town earlier than Rachel had said? She tried to compare the man's voice with Dr. George Brant's, to see if the voices matched. Heart pounding, she hit the redial button and got a busy signal. Probably, they'd taken the phone off the hook. Probably, Rachel was right now entwined with the Wellesley man, her limbs knotted helplessly with his, his expensive suit on a hanger in the closet. *No wonder the "doctor" called*, she thought. *No wonder Rachel accompanied me to the airport and stayed until she was certain I could get a flight.* Together, Rachel and the Wellesley man had probably laughed and laughed as they imagined Beth on a scavenger hunt for a mother who wasn't dying. "Well I had to get her out of the way somehow," Rachel had probably said between giggles. Beth couldn't breathe. The future seemed inscrutable, as if, at the morning's first light, she could quite possibly fall from the earth.

The water pipes grew even louder. She leaned against the cool bathroom wall, her knees pulled in tight. She jammed her fingers in her ears and licked the tears from her cheeks. She wished her head was made of metal so she could bang it against the wall loudly enough to drown out the sound of the pipes. She imagined Rachel and the Wellesley man could see her, that they were watching her in this basement apartment, laughing at her, mimicking the noise by beating pots and pans with metal spoons. But the image of Rachel and the man turned into one of Beth and her mother, long ago, side by side on a gray cement floor, drumming on pots to the rhythm of a clanging radiator and singing, "I've Been Working on the Railroad." Her mother had called it a "concert of heat." Beth was maybe nine years old, so her mother would have been only a few years older than Beth was now, and more beautiful than Rachel or anyone in the world.

Finally, the pipes grew quiet. Beth crept back to bed. She pictured herself on her knees before her mother, her mother's hand on her head. "I had to leave," she would say, "but I've got money for us now. You can have a good life if you'll come back with me."

No time at all seemed to pass before she woke to daylight and the giraffe calling, "C'mon now, Liz Dinard. Get up and pee, the world's on fire."

Rita made toast and sat on the cushions beside Beth's makeshift bed. "You won't have any trouble catching a cab now," she commented as she spread jam on Beth's toast with a plastic butter knife.

"Oh," Beth replied in a voice she hoped sounded casual. "I was thinking that I would stay until I found my mom." But the plan seemed less appealing than it had the previous night. Now she remembered incidents at the grocery store when her mother, in mismatched shoes and a homemade newspaper hat, had screamed at the cashier, "There's no way I'm paying for any of this!" She imagined how Rachel would point out Beth's mother to the Wellesley man, and how he'd laugh, "*That's* what you were involved with? Ugh! What a mess."

"There's the York Motel," Rita said between bites. "As you know."

"Yes." The toast caught in Beth's throat.

"Well you didn't think you were staying on here, did you?" the giraffe said. "I mean, that was for yesterday only. You get that, right?"

Beth felt herself tearfully nodding like a child. "I'm sorry," she sobbed. "I'm just going through this thing."

"Yeah, well we're all going through something." Rita took her plate to the sink. She opened a kitchen cabinet to reveal a stack of maroon bath towels, took the top one, and said, "I gotta work at noon. That gives you a couple-a hours to get yourself together before you hafta go."

Beth listened to the shower water running. The pipes began to moan and clatter again. Go where? There was nowhere. The motel oozed loneliness, so did the prospect of living with her mother again, so did the prospect of living without Rachel. Beth wanted to stay in this basement, rest in the giraffe's arms and eat from her fingers.

The giraffe exited the bathroom fully dressed. "Your turn," she told Beth.

And Beth lowered her head and whispered, "Do you want a back rub?"

She couldn't decide whether Rita's eyes looked tempted or wary.

"Take a shower," she told Beth, "then go."

When Beth was in the bathroom with the door closed and locked, she heard the giraffe say, "A back rub. Jesus Christ."

After her shower, Beth put on the grungy clothes and underwear she'd worn the day before. Then she gobbed toothpaste onto the giraffe's toothbrush and used it. She rinsed the toothbrush then brushed her eyebrows with it. She rifled through the medicine cabinet and used some deodorant. She stole two tampons and put them in the back pocket of her jeans. She noticed an open box of condoms which she emptied into her pockets as well. Then she flushed a handful of the yellow prescription pills down the toilet.

Beth found the giraffe squatting beside the iguana cage. "Thanks for the hospitality," she said as curtly as possible.

"Yeah, sure," the giraffe replied. "Ciao."

Her eyes had adjusted to the dim basement and even the tawny city sunlight hurt. Fuck the giraffe. Fuck her mother. She was going home. She would catch Rachel and the Wellesley man together. But then what? She thought of the fight she'd had with Rachel only two days before. "I can't keep reassuring you, you know," Rachel had finally said. "It's tedious." *You're tedious*, Beth thought now. *Your pity and your ambivalence are tedious, and they make me do tedious things too.* Go home? There was no home. Blinking, she walked to the corner store where she bought a three-pack of panties, a toothbrush, and toiletries. Then she waited for a bus that would take her back to the York Motel.

There was no such thing as before and after. There was no such thing as a whole new life. The only car in the motel parking lot was a rusted-out Pinto without wheels. Holes and discarded butane lighters pockmarked the asphalt, and a dirty mattress spanned two empty parking spaces. *Rachel was right*, Beth decided. *Rock bottom. So, what of it? I've been here before.*

September 1981

With a voice that seemed to slide in and out of tune, the man behind the desk explained the Housing Authority rules. He'd given Angela's eight-year-old daughter, Beth, a plastic puzzle to play with, but to Angela, he said, *No drugs, Miss Dinard, no loud music after ten, no this, no that, no, no.*

No drugs. As though that would solve anything. Angela hadn't taken a damn thing today—Mitch hadn't left a bag for her this morning—and already her body was betraying itself, her bones growing hot, then cold, then hot again. Already, she had begun to see the small, red contaminants that, three years ago, Roz had taught her how to notice. The contaminants, blood red and shaped like kernels of corn, covered the toy Beth held, but Beth, apparently, couldn't see them. Angela watched her daughter play with the puzzle awhile before pausing to pick her dirty cuticles until they bled. Next, Beth mopped the blood with the ends of her ratty hair, shoved the ends of her hair in her mouth, and chewed. Angela looked away. *She can't see poison because she is poison,* Roz often reminded her.

"It's a nice apartment," the man behind the desk said. "I don't know what you've heard about public housing, but this is different. This is nice. You'll see."

Nice is relative, Angela wanted to say, but she nodded instead, showing her gratitude. Showing gratitude for charity was something she'd probably have to get good at now that she wasn't welcome at home. For the last six weeks, since her brother Jimmy's death, and since her mother, presumably grieving over Jimmy, had decided to live alone from now on, Angela and Beth had been staying at Mitch's. But Mitch always had the television blaring because he couldn't hear

Roz talking in the layer of sound that played behind the voices of actors and starlets and newscasters with hairstyles like giant globes. From her place deep within the television, Roz warned Angela of the contaminants. They lived in Mitch's shampoo and refrigerator, and on every inch of Beth's body. Angela had needed to get away. Lately, she'd been leaving in the night to sleep in the park, just for purity and quiet.

"No unattended minors…" continued the man behind the desk. He slid her a paper to sign, and then held out a key, which was crawling with red poison. Angela wouldn't touch it, but her daughter took the key solemnly between bloody fingers as though she and the man had decided to enter into a secret pact.

The man's desk was in an office on a street that had nothing to do with anything Angela needed. The Housing Authority, read the heading on the paperwork. But the promised "housing" was far away from this "authority"—if the man behind the desk was, indeed, the authority—in a part of town in which the "authority" would probably never be willing, himself, to live. And, though it was hard to hear him, hard to keep track of what he said, Angela could feel expenses forming rows of red numbers and knew that, even with the subsidy from the "authority," the food coupons, and the small amount of cash she'd get each month, there would be no way to pay the rent.

Ever since getting pregnant with Beth at sixteen years old, she'd been cleaning apartments for cash—apartments where her mother's friends lived—but those jobs would all dry up now that Jimmy was dead. How awful her mother's friends had been at Jimmy's funeral, whispering about "the drugs" behind their hands, muttering aspersions about Jimmy and Angela in their froggy, old-lady voices. No, they wouldn't welcome her into their homes anymore, even though any given inch of those homes held more contaminants than a year's supply of heroin ever could. And how was she supposed to make money now? What was she supposed to do? Learn to type? She was twenty-four years old, too old to finish high school. Maybe she could work at a school with dozens of kids who picked their fingers and sucked their hair? She couldn't imagine a more dangerous way to spend her time.

I'll show you how to see the poisons, Roz had told her on a hot August day three summers ago, the very first time Angela had heard her voice. Angela was at one of her mother's friend's apartments, sweating as she cleaned the living room. Like Angela's mother, this woman had the television on constantly, probably even when she slept. While her mother's friend sat on the couch, alternately watching a game show and Angela's work, Angela dusted the coffee table, picture frames, and each ceramic statue in the curio cabinets. On the game show, a regular person and a celebrity worked as a pair. The non-celebrity was meant to guess the word "geranium" while the celebrity administered clues, but another voice, Roz's voice, emerged from behind the celebrity's. *The poisons are everywhere,* she said. *I'll show you how to see them.* And Angela saw the red contaminants moving between each surface she dusted and the dust rag she held. She noticed even more of them hanging in the air, heavy red particles illuminated by the television's glow.

"What do I do?" she asked Roz.

"Just finish dusting. Then worry about what's next," answered her mother's friend.

I don't know, Roz said, admitting that she herself was only protected from the contaminants by her pure, clean husband and, even more importantly, her pure, clean daughter who made everyone proud.

"It's a bizarre fixation," her brother Jimmy said, later, when she told him about Roz. "I know people have it about the Kennedys, but that makes some sense. They're like rock stars. Having fantasies about the Carters is just weird." But he, having the same name as Roz's husband, couldn't possibly have understood. Besides, it was Roz who'd sought *her* out; it wasn't a fantasy, like those silly dreams people had about Elvis or the Kennedys. Angela wasn't Roz's fan; she was her confidante.

Perhaps, Angela thought, her brother felt jealous that Roz had chosen *her* when, all their lives, everyone had always chosen Jimmy. But when she looked at Jimmy, she saw there wasn't a single contaminant on him; he was clean and pure and bright as the moon, and she understood. Roz had chosen her, not Jimmy, because she was the one in danger of contamination. So, she felt grateful for Roz and, at first, even hoped for her voice whenever a television played. But three years had passed, and Roz, having been taken from public life last January, now seemed unable to leave Angela alone. Angela wished she could live in a world without television, a world with only books and books and books. And, of course, the gorgeous relief of heroin, which obliterated Roz's voice and the contaminants too, and turned everything as white and pure as Jimmy. Mitch was usually good for that, and, these past weeks, hadn't even charged her, because he felt responsible for Jimmy, who'd died trying to get some cash to pay Mitch.

Now, the man behind the desk gave Angela more papers to sign, carbons of which she was meant to keep. "For your records, Miss Dinard," he said. She almost laughed. Records?

"It should have taken a lot longer than this," the man continued, "what with the waiting lists, but I pushed yours through." And Angela noticed, at last, that the man was looking at her in that way men often did. She saw herself through his eyes, her long, red hair and smooth olive skin that was beginning to flush with the early stages of withdrawal. This was when, strangely, she knew she looked her prettiest. In an hour, she'd look and feel hideous, and any man would be good enough. But for now, she could contemplate him and decide. He didn't appear to be contaminated, but he did appear too soft, too old, and his hair, like her daughter's, was the color of mud.

Jimmy had also had red hair, a preposterous hair color for Sicilian children to have, but there it was. People had always made their mother wince by asking whether Angela and Jimmy were Irish. "Look at their faces," their scandalized mother would answer. "Are those Irish faces to you?" But, even so, that hair color. Sometimes, even now, catching a glimpse of herself reflected in a store window, the beauty of her own hair gave Angela chills.

How gorgeous that color had looked on Jimmy when he lay there at the wake, his hands folded primly as though he were a different person altogether. The quiet, faceless morticians had rouged his cheeks and made up his eyes, and the colors they'd used, so unnatural, emphasized the natural, wonderful luster of his hair. *You couldn't tell he'd ever been shot*, Angela thought, looking at Jimmy, so pure and whole, while Beth pulled on her skirt with those contaminated hands, saying, "Mama, Mama, Mama," her voice a hundred thousand police sirens.

Angela's father had died five years prior, and though he had been a stranger, really, with his newspapers, silence, and big wicker-wrapped jugs of Chianti, when Jimmy died, it was as if she'd lost her father again too—as if every loss stuck to every other loss, the way chewing gum stuck to quarters when she and Jimmy fished for change in gutters when they were small. At the funeral, not long before Jimmy was put into the ground forever, she thought of her lost brother and lost father and then, absurdly, of all the animals she and Jimmy had lost as children. There was the beagle named Baxter, the tabby cat named Bailey, and the orange canary that Jimmy, at age eight, had christened Autumn Leaf. But those animals were all "too dirty" for their mother's comfort. Even the cat, who was supposed to be naturally good at that kind of thing, stood inside the litter box and defecated over the side, onto the utility room linoleum. How their mother cried every time the dog or bird or cat soiled the floor! And soon their father took the animal away—to a farm, their mother always said. But as the priest talked about lost potential, ostensibly to memorialize her brother, Roz spoke to Angela in the cathedral's echoes, telling her there had never been a farm at all, and Angela wept for the poor, lost pets.

Mitch didn't come to Jimmy's wake, not once over the entire two days. He didn't come to the funeral, the burial, or even the small luncheon at her mother's apartment, where Beth ate egg salad sandwiches until Angela's mother said, "Girl, if you eat another one of those, I'm gonna cut off your fingers and feed them to the chickens," at which Beth laughed and laughed.

Angela's mother and daughter had always been close, so close there was no room left for Angela or anyone else. Beth was born a month premature. Angela didn't know about contaminants yet, but she intuited something about Beth, because she had never seen anyone uglier. When Jimmy was first allowed to see the kid in the hospital, he actually laughed over the plastic warmer before asking, "What's wrong with her? She looks like some kind of Martian!"

"Hush your mouth," their mother admonished. "She's gorgeous."

But "gorgeous" couldn't have been less true. Unlike the plump, smooth-skinned, round-headed infants pictured in diaper ads, Beth had scrawny, rickety-looking legs, a pointed head covered in mud-colored hair, and a wrinkled face, like a shar-pei's. A horrible, scaly red rash on Beth's eyelids portended the contaminants, Angela realized later.

"We'll call her Elizabeth," Angela's mother said. "Now we've got lots of royal names in the family. Elizabeth and James."

"And Angie," said Angela.

"You're royal all right," said her mother. "A royal *what*, I hate to say."

"Pain in the ass," Jimmy finished unnecessarily, and he punched Angela's arm until she laughed. Jimmy had always been able to make her laugh. Later, Angela decided it was because of his innate purity.

"What the hell is the matter with you two?" Angela's mother scolded.

Angela hadn't known how she'd feel, of course, when the baby actually came, though she'd suspected she wouldn't feel happy, the way she knew she was supposed to. "Who is he? Who did it?" everyone had demanded, her brother bashing his head into the wall, her mother crying, her father, ordinarily a cipher, peeking out from behind his newspaper to hear. But Angela wouldn't say.

Nine years ago, when her period didn't come, the boy who'd knocked her up brought her to Brooklyn, to the woman his sister had gone to when she had gotten into trouble, but she'd wanted more than a thousand dollars, and they couldn't pay. So, for what a doctor would've charged to take care of everything legally only a year later, the woman gave Angela a plastic bag of herbs to make into a tea, which, she said, might or might not do the trick. That was a Saturday, and the next day, at mass, Angela prayed that, if there was a God, the tea would work. But the tea didn't work, and she never came up with enough money to revisit that woman in Brooklyn. She asked and asked Beth's father until her stomach grew, the boy stopped speaking to her, and it was far too late to ask anymore. There was no God, she decided; otherwise, how could you explain why, despite her mother's prayers and prayers and prayers, she had turned out the way she had.

She'd been nothing but trouble all her life. And how she'd always laughed when her mother tried to punish her. To see her mother arrayed in a seersucker suit and righteous temper, charging toward Angela with a leather strap raised! "Here, I'll do it for you," Jimmy would say, and he'd bang his own head into the wall, hard, and Angela would join him, until their mother collapsed to her knees, sobbing, praying, begging them to stop. "Bad seed," her mother sometimes said. "Born with the Evil Eye, you were."

Beth's father had a new girlfriend by the time Angela got big enough for everyone to notice. Angela saw them necking by the lockers on the first floor of her high school, the high school her mother made her continue attending as she grew bigger, even though she'd have the baby two years before she could graduate. Beth's father didn't have to hear the girls laughing about her in gym class, or the boys who sang, "Is you is or is you ain't my baby?" and grabbed her crotch or breasts when she walked past them in the school hallways. He didn't have to hear the men who whistled at her, after school, as she made her way down the crowded sidewalks to her mother's friends' apartments, to clean places where she'd never live and chop garlic for dinners she'd never eat, while the old women corrected her every move and made it clear that, disgrace that she was, no one but those loyal to her mother would hire her as anything other than a *puttana*.

It was a word she heard a lot during the two days of the wake, the old people's standard, whispered recrimination about "Jimmy's sister." At the wake, the funeral, and over sandwiches at her mother's, the old people looked at her as though certain she'd be the next corpse, and she, looking back at them, saw the poison coating their skin and knew they were wrong. Afterwards, once everyone had gone, her mother turned on the television, and Angela could barely hear her mother's words over Roz's when her mother said, "Get out. I'm done with you. You and Jimmy both. I did everything I could." But Roz explained, *She's poison; don't you see that? She and your daughter, too. That's what really killed Jimmy. They'll say it was drugs that undid him, but that wasn't it at all. It was their poison. You're better off without them. You're safer.*

"Will I still be allowed to visit Beth?" Angela asked her mother despite Roz's urgings.

"Visit her? She's going with you. You're her mother, not me. I'm no one's mother anymore." And she put her head in her hands and cried.

Angela packed her clothes into a duffel bag along with some syringes and cottons she retrieved from under her mattress. Beth's clothes were contaminated, so she put them in a plastic bag before packing them into the duffel, to keep her own clothes pure. She stood with the duffel bag between her feet and waited for her mother to change her mind, but it never happened. Finally, her mother looked up at her with hard eyes and said, "You took your shit, right? The shit under your mattress? Well, you'd better take Jimmy's too. I'm sure you know where he hid it."

When they left, her mother didn't say good-bye to her, only to Beth, to whom she said, "Good luck, Bethie. I hope you can break the curse. God knows I can't."

"What curse, Mama?" Beth asked as they started to walk away. "I didn't hear a curse."

"Your grandmother's the curse," Angela answered. Maybe Beth would be purged of contaminants now that they were on their own, Angela hoped as they walked to Mitch's, the duffel bag heavy on her arm.

Now, however, a television played somewhere in the Housing Authority office, and some bureaucrat or other mentioned that Ronald Reagan had taken down the solar panels Jimmy Carter once installed on the White House roof. From behind the broadcast, Roz hollered, *You hear that? We're all going be poisoned to death now!*

She shivered. On her arms, each fine hair stood in a pool of sweat. The man behind the desk seemed to be looking at her differently. She was starting to lose her prettiness, she knew. "I'm off in about half an hour," the man said. "We're not supposed to, strictly speaking, but I can give you a lift if you like. You look tired."

The pain in her bones had begun to grow and spread, and from the waiting room television, Roz caterwauled: *Ask him if he knows about the solar panels?* Angela couldn't wait half an hour.

"She needs a cigarette," Beth said.

"Here." The man took an ashtray from his desk drawer. Angela had half a pack of Marlboros in her purse and felt a bit calmer when the smoke caught behind her sternum, a nice feeling, like the tightening pull of a loose shoelace. "Last week," she said, blowing smoke, "we got some bus tokens when we picked up our check."

"Sure you don't want a ride?" he asked.

"We have to go get our things," she said. "We can do it on the bus."

Ask him, Roz reminded her. But when Angela obeyed, the man replied curtly, "What does it matter that Reagan took down solar panels? He freed the hostages, didn't he?"

"No," Angela answered.

"Then who did? Not Carter."

"By definition, hostages can be freed only by those holding them," Angela said.

"Iranians," Beth added, sucking the ends of her hair.

And then they were outside, waiting for a bus. Heroin was a strange affair, Angela thought, shivering and sweating, the contaminants so ubiquitous now that they overlaid her vision with an odd crimson cast. At first, it's just about itself, the gorgeous purity it provides, but by the time it's part of your daily life, you're embarrassed of your need for it. Sometimes she wondered whether her need or her embarrassment would last longer.

How wonderful it was that first time! How much like falling in love! When Angela and Beth came home from the hospital, Jimmy handed Beth to their mother, who commandeered the infant instantly, feeding her from a bottle and cooing like an imbecile. When it seemed clear that neither Beth nor Angela's mother had any remaining affection, Angela followed Jimmy, for the very first time, to meet Mitch. "Come on," Jimmy said. "Baby shower time."

Mitch opened his apartment door, his long blond hair loose around his narrow face. "She's pretty!"

"What did I tell you?" Jimmy replied.

But when Mitch brought her to bed and saw the blood, he asked, "When did you have that baby?" And he lifted Angela into his arms as though *she* were the baby and rocked her, saying, "I'm sorry. I'm sorry. I didn't realize," while she cried into his shirt, a howl of despair inside her bigger than the whole world. "Here," said Mitch, and he got the needle ready. "Try it. It'll help. I promise." And it did help. With the needle's first clean penetration, as the quiet, white warmth spread up and down her arms and legs, memories presented themselves to her. She was four years old, stubbing her toe on the sidewalk, and Jimmy, who was only eight, scooped her up in his arms and ran her home, making a siren noise with his mouth. She was five or six years old, and she and Jimmy took turns rolling down the front steps of row houses on Poplar Street in an empty refrigerator box Jimmy had found. During one descent, Angela got something in her eye, and Jimmy sat beside her on the stoop, saying, "Look up," while he pried back her eyelid and extracted a large splinter. She understood, finally, that Jimmy had brought her to Mitch's because he'd wanted to bring her back to the world of childhood, the world in which only she and he existed, the world before Beth.

At Mitch's, away from Beth, Angela's breasts grew engorged with milk and then, some days or weeks later, dried forever. And she thought she just might stay at Mitch's because the sheets on his guest room bed were soft and clean and, in those days, he seemed to love her, calling her, "Sexy Sue" though it wasn't her name, and kissing her eyelids when he came into the guest room to wake her. But, one day, her mother arrived at Mitch's, Beth in her arms, and screamed at Jimmy, "Your sister is sixteen years old! Sixteen!" And she dragged both of them back home.

And it seemed, then, that giving up heroin wouldn't be any problem at all, but Jimmy would ferry it to her, a gift, at first, from Mitch. By the time Mitch seemed to forget her, her body had made an allegiance to it against her will and her bones changed temperature when she tried to stop. Meanwhile, Angela's mother monopolized Beth so egregiously that, when the child first learned to talk, guess who it was that, for almost a full year, she called "Mama"? Today, however, Angela's mother had turned them out, Jimmy was dead, and it was Beth who led the way to Mitch's, where, in the hallway outside his apartment, their duffel bag waited, already packed, presumably by Mitch. But Mitch wasn't home, and without having to be told by Roz or anyone, Angela knew that Mitch was done with her, with both of them. Like her mother, Mitch had enough, and now she was on her own.

By the time they found the bus to lead them to the tenements, it was dark and getting cold, and the back of Angela's eyes felt as though they were coated with thick, red moss. She could barely feel the bus seat beneath her thighs. Soon, Roz would start talking continually, television or not. The bus moved slowly, its brakes shrieking. In the street, people in nearby cars honked horns, waved Mexican flags, and shouted.

"Is it September?" Angela heard herself ask.

"Yes, Mama," Beth answered.

Independence Day, Roz said. *But not yours.*

The car beside the bus had its windows open, and the passengers sat in the window frames, feet inside the car, heads and torsos jutting into the night air. Pretty teenage girls, not all that much younger than she was, smiled in their lipstick and dark ponytails. "Viva Mexico!" they cried. They'd been smart enough not to get themselves pregnant and could therefore enjoy a holiday. Angela wouldn't have holidays anymore, she realized.

At home, their mother had always made dinners for Christmas and Easter, ham and manicotti and sometimes even roast beef. Aunts and uncles and cousins had come, bringing bread and pie and wine.

A meal like that would cost an entire month's worth of food coupons. But even if she could afford to cook like that, and even if she knew how, there'd be no one to invite now that Jimmy was gone.

And invite where? The "authority" had said the housing was nice. "You'll see," he'd promised. But the bus had stopped, they were here, and she saw that the buildings were only U-shaped concrete columns. They made their way to the building to which they were assigned and discovered a broken elevator inside a foyer that smelled of old cooking and urine. They climbed the stairwell's cement steps to the fourteenth floor where the hallway offered more cement and cinder blocks, with a row of apartment doors on one side and a wall made of chain-link fencing on the other. A stiff, mid-September breeze carried the noise from Mexican Independence Day celebrations through the chain-link. *Twenty-four years old,* Roz said, *and this is where you wind up.*

"There's a playground." Beth peered through the chain-link down to the blacktop far below. A lone figure walked among the broken swings; he slumped against the breeze. How she wished he were Mitch, or anyone, really, who'd look at her and know instantly, asking, "You need something?" in that way of someone who knows. But this neighborhood was foreign to her. Even Jimmy had never come here.

She followed Beth down the hallway to the apartment door marked with the number on the housing agreement, and she let Beth unlock the door so she wouldn't have to touch the poisoned key. The tiny, bare apartment was contaminated top to bottom. She thought of her mother's lace curtains and knotted throw rugs, her floor lamps and rooster-patterned kitchen wallpaper. How she'd hated her mother's awful apartment, the narrow two-story row house with the windows closed day and night, the curtains drawn as though trying to beat back the city. How she'd hated the plastic-covered furniture, the plastic tablecloth, and the crucifixes made of palm leaves that hung on every wall. But it was paradise compared to this empty cement box. Here, they didn't even have beds. She hadn't thought of that. "What did we do?" she asked.

Outside, there came the unmistakable, hollow sound of gunshots.

"Fireworks," said Beth, happily.

"That's not fireworks," she answered. Roz shouted, *See? This is just like what happened to your brother. If you get shot next, it's on your mother's head.*

"It's on your grandma's head if I get shot," Angela echoed.

"It's fireworks," Beth insisted.

The hollow sounds continued, along with shouts of "Viva! Viva Mexico!" in the street. Angela's head ached more with every shout, with every car horn, and with every short, hollow blast of gunfire.

"Let's go look at the fireworks, Mama, please?" Beth persisted. Her voice was enough to make anyone want to jump out the window.

"In a minute." She slumped against a poisoned wall, her feet, still pure and clean, extended in front of her. *Listen*, Roz said. *Listen.* And now Angela could hear the police sirens, lots of them, growing louder, coming close.

Visiting Mrs. Ferullo

The steamy warm smell of Mrs. Ferullo's cooking reached through the open apartment windows, down to the curb where Beth Dinard tried to breathe the smell into her stomach. In one hand, Beth held the red plastic handle of the Phillips-head screwdriver she'd stolen from Mario's Hardware. She'd stolen it to make an acorn finger ring for Mrs. Ferullo.

Beth sniffed, took an acorn from her pants pocket, pried off and discarded the brown cap, and rubbed one rounded end of the nut against the concrete curb to sand it flat. She smelled spaghetti sauce. But what was Mrs. Ferullo cooking *with* the spaghetti sauce? Maybe ravioli, meatballs, and garlic bread?

Sanding the acorn left green, sticky residue on the curb and Beth tried to keep her clothes away from the growing green stain. Mrs. Ferullo probably wouldn't invite her inside unless she looked clean and neat. When both ends of the acorn were sanded flat, the shell was a ring-shaped disc filled with green nut-meat. She would need the screwdriver to scrape the disc clean.

Beth jammed the tip of the Phillips head into the center of the nut-meat, dreaming of thick slices of garlic bread with butter-yellowed centers as soft as skin. She was too rough with the screwdriver, and the green, sticky nut-meat didn't come out in a whole piece. Half the meat remained in the shell and the other half landed on her jeans. "Christ, now I got acorn guts all over me." She brushed the chunks of green from her pants; they left streaks on the denim, which she failed to spit-scrub away. "Dammit!" She bit her forearm and counted, by sevens, to eighty-four. She'd have to make a perfect acorn ring if she was going to approach Mrs. Ferullo with green-streaked pants.

With the tip of the Phillips head, Beth cleaned the rest of the acorn-meat from the shell. Without anything inside it, the shell could be worn as a ring. Beth slipped it onto her finger but the ring cracked as it passed over her knuckle. "Dammit!" She stomped on the broken ring, breaking it further until it blended in with the broken glass, old leaves, and gravel along the curbside. With her left heel, she pressed down hard on the toes of her right foot. She took another acorn from her pocket and began the sanding process again. When the second ring was finished, she didn't try it on. With the new ring in one back pocket and the screwdriver in the other, she climbed the seven steps leading to Mrs. Ferullo's front stoop, the smell of spaghetti sauce growing stronger with each step. Inside the building lobby, the smell was dizzying. Being inside Mrs. Ferullo's apartment might be a lot like being inside a loaf of garlic bread—warm and spicy with things to eat all around. On the wall alongside a doorbell, a strip of sticky-backed black plastic bore Mrs. Ferullo's name in raised white letters.

She'd started to love Mrs. Ferullo a month before. School was out for the day and Beth was walking down Pavonia Avenue, looking for a clock so she'd know how much longer she had to wait before the firehouse tested its sirens, as it did at six thirty every evening. *Don't come home until you hear the six thirty whistle*, was her mother's only rule. Earlier that afternoon, Beth's second-grade class had been reviewing times-tables. Although Beth knew the sevens particularly well, her teacher asked a different girl to answer seven times twelve. That student counted on her fingers and answered, "Nineteen."

Before Beth could edit her behavior, her hand shot in the air. "Eighty-four!" she shouted. When the teacher called out a new equation, Beth raised her hand again. Repeatedly waving her hand in the air, she imagined she was a whiz kid on TV whose program was being watched by a nice lady sitting on a living room couch somewhere. The lady pointed to the TV Beth and said, "I like her. She's my favorite." But her teacher snapped, "I see your hand, Beth. Put it down and give someone else a chance!" Beth bit the inside of her lip and counted, by sevens, to eighty four.

When the bell rang, Beth waited for the classroom to empty out then stood in front of her teacher's desk, hoping to be noticed. She was about to say she was sorry when the teacher, without looking up, asked, "Aren't you supposed to be heading home, Beth?"

"I guess," Beth answered, "but..."

"Go home, Beth."

Afterward, walking down Pavonia Avenue, Beth saw Mrs. Ferullo, small and lovely, running toward the front door of the Jersey Market. Beth followed and stared as Mrs. Ferullo rifled through a bin of red onions. Beth had never eaten a red onion and wondered what it would taste like. When her mother went grocery shopping, she always came home with a loaf of white bread, a dozen eggs, and a package of bologna which she fried and served in single-slice helpings. Mrs. Ferullo bought fresh vegetables and flour and sugar and garlic and yeast.

Beth stood behind her in line at the cash register, letting her fingertips brush against the scratchy, brown sweater around Mrs. Ferullo's waist.

"Hello Mrs. Ferullo!" the cashier smiled.

"Good day," she replied. She was paying with cash instead of food stamps, even though her order rang to nearly ten whole dollars. Beth was suddenly afraid Mrs. Ferullo would turn around, see her, and threaten to call the police. While the cashier was putting Mrs. Ferullo's groceries into paper sacks, he looked at Beth and asked, "Are you on line, Miss?"

"Good day," Beth answered.

"Are you buying, Miss, yes or no?"

She didn't know what to say. She didn't want Mrs. Ferullo to turn around and ask why she was on line empty handed, but she didn't want to give up her place behind her either. She asked the cashier, "Do you know how to make macaroni and cheese?"

"Of course."

"I don't mean the kind in the box. I mean the kind in the oven. I mean *that* kind."

"If I had the recipe, I bet I could."

"If I was a grown-up," Beth said, "I'd know how to make it without the recipe."

Mrs. Ferullo's groceries were now fully bagged and Beth followed her outside. She wanted to offer to carry her bags, but Mrs. Ferullo moved too fast and, even running, Beth couldn't catch up to her. But she wasn't too far behind to learn where Mrs. Ferullo lived. Half an hour later, she knew it was Mrs. Ferullo's cooking that she smelled. She recognized the garlic.

Since then, she'd been preparing to meet Mrs. Ferullo. She stole a cookbook and tried to learn its recipes by heart because her meeting with Mrs. Ferullo would undoubtedly end up in the kitchen. Today, on her way to Mrs. Ferullo's apartment building, Beth collected acorns and stopped into Mario's Hardware for the screwdriver. *I'll meet her today before the six thirty whistle,* Beth promised herself. For once, she would not be sitting on the hallway floor outside her mother's apartment at exactly six thirty. Instead, she would saunter into the apartment at seven or even seven thirty and, when her mother, crying and reading in the windowside chair, finally looked up from her book, Beth could announce, "I've been visiting Mrs. Ferullo."

Then, when her mother sighed, "I suppose you're hungry," Beth could say, "I'm all right. I already ate." And her mother wouldn't mutter, "Well come on then," as she slammed down her book and turned off the living room lights. Beth wouldn't have to squat against the kitchen radiator, her eyes fixed on the tip of her mother's cigarette which was the room's only light and grew long over a skillet of frying bologna until its ash threatened to drop into the food. She wouldn't have to hope that her mother remembered to take the cigarette from her mouth to flick the ash into the sink. And her mother wouldn't say, "Get the tomato out of the fridge, Beth." And Beth wouldn't have to look in the refrigerator for the tomato that was never there. She wouldn't have to watch her mother's face, the cigarette still in her mouth, disappear into the refrigerator and then come out looking different. And her mother wouldn't say, "Isn't that strange. I could've sworn…" in the voice that had to be and yet was not quite hers.

Now, standing in Mrs. Ferullo's brightly lit, spicy-scented lobby, Beth took the perfect acorn ring from her pocket. She cleared her throat and practiced, "Excuse me, Mrs. Ferullo." Her voice was too loud! She repeated the phrase, trying, as she did, to be like one of the quiet girls at school—the girls who didn't yell out the seven times-tables. It was not enough to have a perfect acorn ring; Mrs. Ferullo probably wouldn't open the door for a girl who wasn't shy and quiet. "Excuse me, Mrs. Ferullo," Beth whispered. But it still wasn't enough somehow and she didn't ring the doorbell. Instead, she backed down the front steps, into the middle of the street. She would only ring the doorbell if she could clear all seven of Mrs. Ferullo's front steps with a single running leap.

Beth shook out her arms and took deep breaths; on TV, runners did that before they raced. Today, if she was finally invited upstairs, Mrs. Ferullo might ask her to get the tomato out of the fridge and there would be seven or eight to choose from. She sprinted toward the steps very fast—fast enough, in fact, to be one of those TV runners. She played background music in her head and imagined Mrs. Ferullo watching, pointing to the TV version of Beth and saying, "I like her. She's my favorite."

Beth jumped. The toes of her right foot landed on the stoop, but her right heel and entire left foot landed in the air somewhere between the stoop and the seventh step. She couldn't save herself from falling and slid backward down the steps, making new holes in her jeans. "Dammit!" The screwdriver poked into her lower back and she counted, by sevens, to eighty-four.

Knees stinging, she backed into the street again. Mrs. Ferullo probably had a needle and thread and might even be able to teach her how to stitch. She might teach her, that is, if Beth remembered to ask for help in her new shy and quiet voice. Mrs. Ferullo probably had soap too and, once she saw the perfect acorn ring Beth had made for her, might not mind helping her wash the acorn guts off her pants. If only she could jump over all seven steps! *And* if she could do it before the six thirty whistle sounded.

Beth charged at the steps and, this time, cleared all of them. "TA DAA!" She hopped up and down, arms over her head, and imagined Mrs. Ferullo clapping for her favorite TV character's victory. Then it occurred to her that she wasn't at all acting like her new shy and quiet self; that, in fact, she'd forgotten all about that new self. Mrs. Ferullo probably wasn't clapping; she was probably shaking her head, turning off the TV, and saying, "What a big mouth!"

Inside the building lobby again, Beth ran her finger over the raised plastic letters that spelled Mrs. Ferullo's name. "Excuse me, Mrs. Ferullo, I made you something," Beth practiced. She picked at the corner of the black plastic strip until it lifted halfway, counted backward, by sevens, from eighty-four to zero, then used the screwdriver to finish peeling Mrs. Ferullo's name off the wall. She folded the name in half and put it in her back pocket with the acorn ring. Maybe it was too much to ask to be invited inside for dinner. Maybe, instead, she could offer the acorn ring, and ask for two tomatoes. Then, tonight, Beth and her mother could sit on the kitchen floor with the lights on and bite into the tomatoes as though they were apples.

The six thirty whistle sounded.

"Dammit!" Beth cupped her hands over her ears, pressing her thumbnails into the fleshy backs of her pointers. When the siren ended, she watched the blood seep through the crescent shaped indentations her thumbnails had made. Sniffing the spicy lobby air, she sucked the blood from her fingertips. Then she remembered tomatoes in baskets outside a storefront on Hutton Street. It would be easy enough to steal a couple on her way home; she didn't need to bother Mrs. Ferullo. At the corner of Hutton Street, Beth dropped the screwdriver and Mrs. Ferullo's name down a rain gutter. The name must have been too light to make much noise as it landed because she could only hear the screwdriver clattering down to join whatever world lived below the street.

Where We're Going This Time

Mama woke Beth before daylight had a chance to scatter the roaches. Her hair was pulled into bunches all over her head, and she wore the purple wrap-around skirt she only wore on movie dates. She said, "Look how much I already did without you. Come on now, Beth, you gotta help." Their duffel bags were filled to bulging on the floor next to Mama's feet.

"Are we going?" But Beth knew the answer to this already, so she started rolling up her bedcovers.

"Never mind with that," Mama said. "We're gonna have new beds where we're going this time."

Beth was glad to be moving early in the day for once. Today, at school, it was her turn to lead the lunch line. To get the good food, you had to be at the front of the line, and Mary Langan, who was in Beth's fifth-grade class and who claimed to love Tater Tots even more than she loved her own Ma, promised to trade her cola-flavored lip-gloss for Beth's place. Even though her Ma told her not to, Mary traded something every day. Beth wondered what Mary would do when she ran out of the things she had.

It smelled good outside, like burning leaves, and they were out even before the vegetable carts. They walked by Mr. Dwayne who was sleeping in the doorway outside Shop n' Go, and Mama nudged his leg with her foot. "We're going, Dwayne."

"Leave me be." Mr. Dwayne didn't open his eyes because he thought they were the cops.

"We're going," Mama repeated. "Don't say I didn't tell you." Then they walked on, Mama wiping her eyes and muttering, "Apeneck Sweeney, that's who he is." Beth knew that poem because Mama knew poems and recited them aloud. And Beth was sad for Mr. Dwayne, and his long arms and silly laugh, and his life that would never get better.

They walked a long time. Beth's duffel bag straps made stripes in her arm skin. She moved the straps and felt the marks. They felt softer than the rest of her skin.

"Where's the new place?"

"You'll see."

But what she saw was the maze of ropes in the bus-station line, and a million people waiting, and Mama's backside in front of her, hips swinging when she stood on one foot, then the other, then the first foot again. There was only one person working there, an old man, and he didn't speak Spanish, so it was taking him a long time to sell tickets.

"Where are we going? Are we leaving Jersey City?"

Mama didn't turn around. "Quiet now, Beth. No questions."

Beth sat on her duffel bag. Finally it was Mama's turn. She said, "Guard the luggage." Beth waited at the front of the maze with the bags between her feet while Mama talked to the old man in Spanish, even though they were Sicilian, not Mexican or Puerto Rican. Mama did this at the post office and at AFDC too, whenever someone working only spoke English. Mama said, "It's a crying shame to only speak your own language." She was teaching Beth the Sicilian she'd picked up from her family and the Spanish she'd learned from the neighborhood. They played Language sometimes; Mama said the English word and Beth tried to give her the words for it in other languages. On bad days, Mama cried when Beth made mistakes and told her that she'd inherited her father's bad brains.

The bus they were taking was empty except for them and some old people who Mama said were probably headed down to Atlantic City. Beth asked if that was where they were going too, but Mama wouldn't answer. Instead, she leaned close to the bus driver and said, "You can get us down the shore without putting us on the Turnpike or Parkway, right? I can't stomach those big highways."

"Have a seat," he answered. And Beth wondered what to expect, whether Mama would yell, "Stop the bus!" as soon as they got onto a highway. Maybe in an hour or so they'd be waiting for the local bus back home with Mama crying, "I just can't do it, Beth. I just can't ride on those big roads," as if it was Beth's fault they'd taken the bus in the first place. By the time Mama stopped crying, Beth thought, it would probably be too late to go to school, and she wouldn't get to lead the lunch line or get Mary Langan's lipgloss.

But none of that happened. The bus hit the Turnpike and Mama said, "Dammit, that imbecile," but she said it quietly enough for only Beth to hear, and then she took Beth's hand and squished her fingers together until they were pins and needles. When they went from the Turnpike to the Parkway, Mama let go of her hand and put her fingers in her ears; her eyes were half shut and her face was red. Beth traced the stripes on the scratchy cloth of the seat in front of her, seeing how many fingers wide each stripe was. Or she looked past Mama out the window. On the Turnpike, there were billboards that, according to kids at school, had dirty pictures hidden in them, but they went by too fast and Beth didn't find anything. On the Parkway, there was only low, brown grass and pine trees on the side of the road. In some places, fires had burned the trees black and in half.

"What are you doing?" Mama noticed Beth's fingers tracing the seat stripes.

Beth shrugged.

"Inarticulate. Spell and define, please."

Beth shrugged again. Mama had her ears plugged anyhow. The old man sitting in front of them had a pink head with brown spots and some dry white hair sticking up like the highway grass. Beth couldn't figure out whether his head had fifteen or sixteen spots because she always forgot which one she started counting on.

"Inarticulate," Mama repeated. "I-N-A-R-T-I-C-U-L-A-T-E. Or do you prefer 'dumb'?"

Beth tried again, reminding herself that spot number one was at the bottom, right where the hair started. She thought that it would be nice to be tiny enough to live on his head, hiding in his hair like it was a cornfield, and all his spots would be her footprints.

"Dumb," Mama said. "D-U-M-B. The B is silent. B, as in Beth. The silent Beth. Or do you prefer 'dumb,' Beth?" Even with her ears plugged, Mama could keep her voice so quiet.

"I prefer dumb," Beth answered.

"Yes," Mama agreed. "That's just as I thought."

Then the bus turned off the Parkway, and Mama smiled. She took Beth's hand in her hand and started thumb wrestling and letting Beth cheat with her pointer. And her voice was loud again and she sang that song, "Come Saturday morning, I'm going away with my friend," but those were the only words she knew, so she sang them over and over until the old man with the spotted head peeked over the back of his seat and gave them the Evil Eye. And then they were giggling like Beth and Darla Santiago did on the lunch line whenever they were allowed to stand together. Darla Santiago had a three speed bike she let Beth ride, and six toes on her left foot. The extra one didn't really look like a toe; it looked more like an earlobe, only smaller. Also, it stuck out all alone in this weird place on the side of her foot. Darla had once explained that she had to buy extra, extra wide shoes for the foot with six toes, and regular shoes for the other foot. Mama said that if Darla had been born in America, the doctors would've cut her sixth toe off as soon as she was born. Mama said America has never had the patience for defects.

They got off the bus at a station on a highway called Route 37. "We're gonna have to cab it," Mama said. "We're still a town away." But there were no cabs waiting at the bus station in whatever town they were in, and there were no people waiting for the next bus to anywhere. There was only a parking lot with rows and rows of cars so shiny that someone had to be selling them. There was a tiny white house too, but the door was shut with a padlock and bore a hand-written sign that read STATION CLOSED. PAY FARE ON BOARD.

Beth sat on a bench guarding the luggage while Mama fiddled with the pay phone stuck to the wall of the house. Gulls pecked at the gravel on the side of the curb; they were big like pigeons, but with longer bodies and beaks. It was the quietest place in the world. When

Mama came to the bench, she had tears all over her face. "Oh, Beth, this was such a mistake," she said. "This was such a *huge* mistake."

"Why?"

"Why? Why! Look where we are, Beth! Just look around you! This is piney country! This is where people marry their first cousins and keep chickens in their backyards."

"They don't have cabs?"

"Of course they have cabs. Don't be an idiot. This has nothing to do with cabs." And she sat on the bench too, crying the kind of crying Beth knew better than to ask questions about. Beth played balance beam on the curb and waited. Every once in a while, Mama's voice squeaked loud. She had her arms all wrapped around herself, and rocked back and forth.

It took a long time before their cab came, and it was a green car not a yellow one. The driver held a cigarette between his teeth, and the inside of his car was hot and smelled like baby throw-up. Beth sat in the back with the bags and Mama sat in front because the driver patted the passenger seat and said, "Come sit by me."

"We come from the city," Mama told him as the cab pulled out of the bus station. "In the city, you never sit in front with the driver."

"That a fact?" the driver asked, and he turned the meter on.

The highway was three lanes with dark pavement that looked smooth, like it would feel like driving on ice cream, but really it didn't feel any better than any other road. Outside, there were stores and restaurants, and cars and car lots, and more stores and more restaurants. Beth couldn't see anybody walking. No kids were outside double-Dutching and no moms carried grocery sacks down the street. In the front seat, Mama leaned her forehead against the window, and Beth saw tears on the side of her face.

"You got chickens?" Beth asked the driver.

"Beth!" Mama reached backward through the gap next to her seat and gave Beth's leg a hard pinch. "We're from the city. She thinks all country folk have chickens."

"Country?" the driver laughed. "No one's had chickens around here for a long time. But if you go west about forty-five minutes, there are some horse ranches. You like ponies?"

"No."

"She's eleven," Mama said. "She's too old for ponies."

"I got a daughter who's twelve," the driver replied. "She's nuts about horses. Unicorns too."

Mama gave Beth a what-did-I-tell-you-about-this-town look over her shoulder.

"But, it's better than being nuts about boys," the driver sighed. "Still, those years are coming up fast enough. Don't know what I'll do then." He turned on the radio. It was a station they got at home, and it came in fine. They hadn't gone as far as it felt like they had, then.

"I got a friend that loves unicorns," Beth said.

"Who, Beth?" Mama said like she didn't believe it. "Who do you know who loves unicorns?"

"Darla."

"Darla," Mama repeated, like it was a curse word. Then, to the driver, she said, "Darla doesn't love anything but herself."

"Stuck-up, huh?"

"Haughty," Mama replied, "with nothing to be haughty about."

Beth kept quiet because she didn't know what haughty meant, though she knew from Mama's voice it was something bad. The restaurants and stores out the car window were different now. Instead of burger places and shoe stores, there were seafood restaurants and places selling bait, tackle, and crabbing cages. The stoplights came more and more often, and there were some small houses and a trailer park with actual people sitting outside their trailers on the kind of plastic chairs they sold at the drug store back home. The cab meter ticked so slowly, it was only up to three dollars. Back home they had hardly ever taken cabs, but when they had, three dollars hadn't even gotten them around the block.

Up ahead, there was a narrow bridge and no buildings at all to look at, only a few bareheaded trees and telephone poles. The water under the bridge was calm and brown-green, and there were some boats and a lighthouse far away.

"They're gonna be building a new bridge this winter," the cabby said. "One high enough they won't have to open it when the sailboats come through."

"Is that the ocean?" Beth asked, but she knew quickly that it wasn't because Mama's hand was pinching at her leg again.

The cabby laughed again. "Ocean? That's the bay. The ocean's got waves. But it's not too far. Crack your window and you can smell the salt." The wind was loud and cold through the open car window, and the smell wasn't salt; it was fish.

"Phew," Mama said. "Close that window."

"You better get used to that smell," the cabby warned. "This whole island smells like that during the off-season. How long you planning on staying?"

"Just for the weekend," Mama answered, but her last word stopped itself because it was only Tuesday, and she'd just tripped herself up with the lie. "I mean, *through* the weekend."

"Odd time to visit," the cabby said. "Only thing still open's the merry-go-round. It's indoors so they don't close it, but I guess you can walk around the beach if you got your winter coats on. You said the Shoreline Motel?"

Mama nodded.

"You gotta be careful there, you know. It's full of transients as soon as the weather turns. Lots of Spanish come in from God knows where."

"From Spain?" Mama asked, her voice narrow.

"I don't know where they're from. Mexico, I wouldn't wonder. Maybe Cuba."

"Then they're not Spanish. The Spanish are from Spain."

The driver didn't talk back. Hardly anyone talked back when Mama had her intelligent voice going, not even Darla who could talk back to almost anyone. But at the next stoplight, the cabby looked at Mama pretty hard. "Those bags you got sure are heavy."

"Yes," Mama agreed. "I've hidden some Spaniards in them. They didn't have enough cash to pay the cab fare."

They got to the motel without anyone saying another word. The cabby charged five dollars, and didn't help take the bags out of the car even though he helped to put them in. Once they were out, he opened his window and said, "There's no buses here, you know. Closest grocery store's three miles. You're gonna need a cab from time to time. Winter's cold right next to the ocean like this. Hard weather for walking in." Then he pulled away.

Mama stood staring after the cab, her eyes squinty either from anger or crying, but it was hard to tell. She patted the top of Beth's head. Crying, then. "You must be tired, Beth. That was a long trip for a little girl."

"I'm not little." The motel was a one-story L-shaped building with a slanted roof like a house and doors numbered one through twelve. At the end of the short branch of the L there was a glass door next to a big glass window with the sign OFFICE hanging in it.

"I phoned," Mama told the man behind the desk. He looked at them the way the cops back home sometimes did.

"Winter rental?" he asked, but he already seemed to know 'cause he handed Mama a clipboard.

"What's this?" Mama pointed to something on the page.

"The TV fee."

"I'm not paying five dollars a week for a TV I won't watch."

"Watch it or not, you've got one in your room, and it's five dollars a week."

"Then take it out of my room, and take it off my bill."

In the corner, there was a fake plant and a candy bar and soda machine. Everything in the machine cost fifty cents. That was way more than things cost at Darla's dad's store back home; his candy and soda only cost a quarter, and he had more choices. Here, everything was chocolate and Coke.

"They don't have any suckers," Beth told Mama. The desk man was stooped over behind the counter, and Mama was just standing there.

"What?"

Beth pointed to the vending machine. "No sours."

"Well that's a tragedy," Mama answered.

"I'm just saying."

"You eat too much junk anyway."

The desk man stood back up and handed Mama a great big key. "She need one too?"

"Well, you don't think she's going to be sleeping in the parking lot, do you?"

"I thought you could maybe share."

"God, what is with this town? Everyone's so literal!"

The desk man smiled at her with wet lips. He was skinny and short and his hair was almost gone. "We've got irony," he said, "if you know where to look."

"How old are you?" Mama asked, smiling now too.

"Young enough," he answered, and his lips got wetter.

"We'll see," Mama said.

Mama and the desk man looked at each other and their big silence made the whole room feel different. Beth didn't know where to stand or what to look at. "Mama?" she said.

Mama looked at Beth and her shoulders got lower and round. "Come on, Beth," she sighed. "Let's go to our room."

"What happened with the TV?" Beth dragged her duffel bag across the parking lot.

"He took it off the bill. Pick that thing up. You're going to put a hole in it."

"So we're not gonna have a TV?"

"I didn't say that." Mama was smiling.

They were in Room 8. It was bigger than Beth thought it would be, and nicer, and there was stuff about fishing everywhere. There was a big plastic fish hanging on a board on the wall, and the wallpaper and the bedspreads had fish designs on them. The lamps looked like tiny crabbing cages with lampshades, and there was a real live ship-in-a-bottle on top of the TV. There were two beds, both big, and a tiny refrigerator. Mama opened her duffel bag and took out the hotplate she brought. "There," she said, putting it on top of the refrigerator.

"The kitchen." Then she untied her wrap-around skirt and let it fall to the floor. She took off her blouse and her slip. She lay belly-down on the bed in her undies and started crying again, loud, the way little kids cried.

"I feel dark days coming, Beth," she said. "Who's gonna help me when they come?"

"I'll help you." Beth wanted this to be true but she knew that she wouldn't be the one, that she didn't have the right kind of help to give. Not like Uncle Derek, who used to come around back home with money and needles. Not even like the man in the office with the wet lips. Maybe he would be the one. She looked through Mama's duffel bag for the rubbing alcohol and cotton balls, but they weren't there. "*Your* bag, Beth!" Mama said, her face still buried in the pillows.

Beth let a cotton ball soak up some alcohol, then sat on the bed beside Mama and rubbed down her back with it. When Beth finished with her back, she got another cottonball ready and did Mama's arms, then her legs, then her feet. The bottoms of her feet were always orange, like Beth's were, and neither one of them knew why that was. Last, Beth used the cotton ball to wash between all Mama's fingers. Beth's hands were almost the same size as Mama's because Mama's were so tiny. Mama always said Beth's hands were too big, like Beth's father's were. Beth tried to hide them from Mama sometimes, because sometimes how big they were made her cry.

By the time Beth finished with her hands, Mama wasn't crying anymore. She held tightly to Beth's wrist. "Sit here while I sleep?"

Beth nodded. "I will, Mama."

There was music playing in the room next door. It sounded like piano music being played on a real piano, and an old man's voice was singing to it. He was singing, "Daisy, Daisy."

"Mama."

"Sssshhhhh!"

"Mama, somebody's got a piano."

"It's a motel, Beth. No one brings a piano to a motel. Now be quiet. My head is splitting." Mama didn't let go of Beth's wrist until she was fast asleep. She looked like someone in the movies with her smooth skin and shiny hair. Next door, the piano music kept going, and the same old man's voice kept singing. Now it was a song Beth didn't know, something about a dead girl. She pressed her ear to the wall, but as soon as she did, the music stopped. There was quiet and a toilet flushed; then the music started again, back at the beginning of the song, and the words that she could hear were, "Where did you go, my fair, my sweet? Where did you go, my lady?" When the music stopped, the night was so quiet it was impossible for Beth to sleep.

In the morning, she woke before Mama, but it was already too late to go to the new school where she was supposed to sign up and maybe even start today. She couldn't turn on the TV and there was no food in the fridge, and she didn't have any money to go to the vending machines in the office. Mama would probably sleep all day, and she'd probably have one of those fevers she always got the day after moving. Beth leaned close to Mama's face and felt her forehead. It wasn't warm, but Mama's fevers never showed on her skin. The curtains were so thick and heavy that there was no sunlight and no air.

Beth put on her coat and sat on the concrete stoop outside their room. There were only planes in the big sky but their noise was too far away to hear. There weren't many cars on the street, and no trucks, and nobody selling anything, and no people walking. The air was cold and wet and smelled like fish, and the sun was white and tiny, like an egg. *Right now*, Beth thought, *Darla and Mary and the other girls back home are probably having recess on the blacktop. They're probably double-Dutching and putting hexes on the boys.* There was no music coming from the old man's room, and Beth didn't want to knock on his door because she needed to listen for when Mama woke up. Finally, the motel office man walked across the parking lot to his car. It was a nice car, shiny and blue, and he waved and shouted, "How's the TV?"

Beth put a finger to her lips so he'd know that Mama was still sleeping. He was only gone a short time, and came back carrying a brown paper sack.

"Locked out?" he asked.

She shook her head, showing him the key she'd already strung around her neck.

"Aren't you cold out here?" His lips didn't look so wet now, and the sunlight made the tiny bit of hair he had look red.

"My Ma's still sleeping."

"I got some sandwiches. You can sit in the office with me and have one."

"No, thank you."

"Suit yourself. You want a sandwich anyway? You can just sit here and eat it and I'll let you be."

She wanted to say yes, but her head wouldn't move. This was always how it started with Mama's friends. They always started by giving Beth things, then they gave things to both Mama and Beth and Beth started calling them "Uncle so-and-so," then it was gifts to Mama and not to Beth, then nothing to either of them and Mama spent her days crying and saying, "Uncle so-and-so won't be coming around anymore."

"I've got tuna and I've got turkey."

"I like salami."

"Well, I don't have salami. I have tuna or turkey. If you want one, say it now because I've got to get back to work."

"Okay. Tuna."

He handed over the sandwich. It was wrapped in clear plastic and tape that was hard to rip open. "Here," he said, and gave her the turkey sandwich too. "Give that one to your mother."

"Thanks."

"Be sure you tell her who you got them from?"

"I know."

"You won't forget?"

"No."

"All right then. If you get thirsty, come on in the office and I'll give you some Cokes."

"Thanks."

Inside the old man's room, the piano music started again. Beth wanted to call out to the office man and ask whether she was hearing things or not, but she didn't know his name, and Mama hated it when she heard Beth yell, "Hey!" or "Yo!"

The old man's window curtains were drawn tight, but there was a tiny gap Beth could almost see through when she stood on tiptoe, and she was balancing there when the music stopped and, through the glass, a blinking eye met hers.

Beth jumped, startled, and backed away from the window, but the door to the old man's room opened and he wasn't at all scary standing in his doorway in his brown pants and light blue shirt and black, fancy socks.

He stretched his arms to both sides, like a scarecrow, and sang, "You like Broadway?" His voice was loud and his teeth looked white and big, like sticks of chalk.

Beth put a finger over her lips. "My mama," she said, pointing toward the door to Room 8. "She's asleep."

The old man nodded his head up and down very fast. "Children should never wake their mamas."

"I won't."

The man disappeared into his room. It felt colder outside now, and Beth wondered if she could ask the man to let her come in and listen to his music.

He came back outside before Beth had the chance to knock on his door. He handed her a crumpled piece of paper. "You know who this is?"

It was a newspaper picture of a girl about her own age with curly hair and a big smile; she was wearing a lace dress and party shoes. Beth shook her head.

"That's Kerry Smith! She's on Broadway!" The old man snatched the newspaper back from Beth. "She's a big star! Everyone loves Kerry Smith."

"She's an actress?"

"An actress! A singer *and* a dancer! She's the biggest star!"

"Do you know her?"

The old man nodded his head up and down again; then he changed his mind and shook it from side to side. "I sing," he said.

"You got a piano in there, don't you?"

"Who told you?"

"I heard you playing it. It's pretty."

"Pretty," the old man repeated. "You sing?"

Beth shook her head.

"You gotta sing," he told her. "If you wanna be a big star, you gotta sing. And dance. It's not enough just to be an actress."

"I'm not gonna be a big star," Beth answered. "My mama could be, though."

"Your mama?" The old man rubbed his hands together. "They don't want mamas. They want young kids. The young kids nowadays, that's what they want. Little girls and little boys. *You* have to be the big star. Make a lot of money for your mama. Keep your mama in the lap of luxury."

"But I can't do anything," Beth said, but even as she said it she imagined what it would be like to be able to give Mama the right kind of help. To buy a house for Mama. A house they would never have to leave.

"Oh now." The old man's voice stretched out long into a silly growl. "You can. You can. You just gotta know how to make all the big shots fall in love with you! That's what these kids have to do nowadays. Just know how to talk!"

"I know poems," Beth said. "My mama teaches me. And different languages too."

"No," the old man said. "No, they don't want poems. Not if you're gonna be a big star! Just give them a 'yes sir' and a 'no sir.' That's what they want! They want someone to give them a pretty curtsey and say, 'Okay!'" He held onto the doorjamb with one large, spotted hand and slowly bent down into a curtsey. "Okay!" He looked at Beth and smiled like the little girl in the newspaper. "Okay!" he said again. "You try."

"Me?"

"Go ahead. Be a big star."

Beth laid Mama's turkey sandwich on the ground, put one foot behind her, spread out her arms, dropped into a low curtsey. She looked at the old man. "Okay?"

"No no no. Too serious! You gotta be cute and happy. That's what they want!" He curtseyed again, smiled big, said, "Okay!"

Beth curtseyed quicker this time, not as low. She imagined standing in the spotlight on a vast, bright stage. The audience looked at her, bags of money in their laps. She made herself smile. "Okay!"

"Atta girl!" The old man clapped his hands together.

Beth did it again and again. "Okay," she said, "Okay!" She felt warm and light. She and Mama could wear party dresses covered in gold coins. They could eat at restaurants and go on trips to the ocean in the summertime when there was more than just the carousel running. It would just be the two of them, just Beth and Mama, because Mama wouldn't need to make friends with so many men.

"Bravo!" The old man started curtseying again too. He took a turn, then Beth did, then he did, then Beth did. "You got what it takes," the old man said. "What's your name?"

"Beth."

"No, no," the old man said. "That's your old name. Your new name is Kerry. Everyone loves Kerry, okay?"

"Okay!" Beth answered, curtseying again. She made her voice squeak a little bit when she said, "Okay," like Darla Santiago did at home sometimes when she was trying to sweet talk her dad into giving her some candy from the store.

"That's it, Kerry!" The old man smiled. "That's the way to do it, Kerry!"

Beth was in the middle of another "Okay," when, from inside Room 8, Mama's voice screamed her old name.

"Where *were* you? My god, where *were* you?" Mama stood on top of her bed, naked and shivering.

"Outside."

"Why?"

"I don't know. You were asleep." Beth wanted to tell Mama all about her new name and Broadway and the movies and money, but it wouldn't do any good because her eyes were someone else's eyes today. "That guy from the office gave us sandwiches. Here. It's turkey."

"Did you eat one?"

"Yeah. Tuna."

"You ate it? Oh, Beth. He might have put something in it. He could have put a mickey in it. I'm not eating mine. These are different people down here, Beth. These people know things about us. They watch us and they know things about us."

Beth curtseyed the way the old man taught her and made herself smile. "Okay!" It still felt good, like she was a different girl, like this was all part of a play. Then she put Mama's sandwich in the fridge because Mama would be hungry when she came back to herself.

"What are you doing?" Mama screamed. "Throw it out! Throw it *out!*"

"Okay!" Beth smiled and curtseyed again. In her head, the audience applauded. She pretended to throw the sandwich out even though she didn't really do it.

Mama watched the curtsey, and her eyes went soft. "Do that again," she said.

Beth curtseyed, smiled. "Okay!" Again, applause welled in her ears.

Mama seemed close to smiling, but then she sighed and looked away. "Silly girl," she said, but she didn't sound angry.

"Are you warm enough, Mama?"

Mama knelt down on the bed and got under the covers. "What have we done, Beth? What kind of wasteland have we landed in?"

"It's okay."

Mama pulled Beth's head against her knees and combed her hair with long fingernails. "I remember when I was just a silly little girl too. I remember having fun, just like you are now, but I don't remember what it feels like anymore. What's it like, Beth? What's it like to have fun?"

Beth tried to imagine herself on the big stage again, but the applause wouldn't come. She tried to imagine the house and the party dresses and the summertime trips to the shore, but she only saw the motel office man holding up a turkey sandwich, reminding her to tell Mama where it came from. "I don't know," Beth answered, and Mama's fingers stopped moving and dug hard into her scalp.

"What do you mean you don't know?" Mama whispered, but it was worse than if she'd shouted it.

Beth kept quiet.

"Don't you dare say that you don't know," Mama kept whispering. "Don't you dare feel sorry for yourself like that."

Beth could feel the sandwich crumbs sticking in her throat. She imagined the motel office man again. Now he was holding up a can of Coke. If he had needles too, he'd have all the right things, it seemed. Beth's back shook, just once. Then Mama started scratching her head again, and Beth's throat relaxed, open and round. Mama said, "I don't mean it, Beth."

"It's okay."

"No. No, it's not. I could kill myself I'm just so sorry."

"It's okay, Mama. Really. It's okay."

"That's a girl. That's a girl. Mama has to sleep awhile now, Beth. Mama needs to rest so the dark won't come again."

Beth stood, pulled the covers around Mama's shoulders, and Mama took both sides of her face, brought Beth's lips down to where hers were and gave her a long kiss. "Stay until I'm sleeping?" she said into Beth's mouth, and everything seemed possible again. After Mama fell asleep, Beth decided, she'd go back to the old man's room and ask him what she needed to learn next. She curtseyed like a big star and smiled at Mama. "Okay."

"Oh Beth." Mama pulled away, rolling over on one side. "Stop saying okay all the time. It makes you sound like an idiot."

O Street

The O Street Girl came back to school today. She arrived between the first and second homeroom bells. She'd been absent since last January, and now it was October, and so many things had happened, things you would have told her once, before she was the O Street Girl, when she still was Beth Dinard, your friend. But no one was talking to her today, so you couldn't tell her about your first French kiss, your first hit off a joint, your first fistfight. No one was talking to her and no one was talking to each other and so much happened since she went away.

The O Street Girl was what the papers called her, because it happened on Oak Street and because they wanted to protect her identity in the world outside this city. But that was many months ago, and the world outside this city soon forgot her. You almost forgot her too; you began to blot her from memory in the way you blotted out other friends of yours who had died. You were fourteen years old and not dead. Last Friday, in back of the Oak Street basketball court, behind the place in the fence where the chain link is most gnarled, Neal Lenard put his tongue into your mouth. You told all your friends about this, about the hard press of his teeth against your lips, and how you could taste the pizza he'd eaten for supper. But you did not tell the O Street Girl, and now she was sitting at a desk in the back row with her head pointed toward her lap, and she was wearing a stupid knit hat that covered her ears, and it seemed as if she was trying to hide from you and from everyone else.

You met her the way you met all of your friends; she was simply there as you were, and as you'd all always been. Before becoming the O Street Girl, she'd sat on the stoops with you, jumped rope with you, played Manhunt on your team. When you smuggled your mother's copy of the *Joy of Sex* into the empty garage on the corner of Oak Street and read parts of it aloud to your friends, it was the O Street Girl who'd never before heard the term "hard." She'd said, "Hard with what? Some kind of coating?" And everyone had laughed because, even though none of you knew very much about sex, you at least knew what caused an erection. But now the O Street Girl knew more and she knew it firsthand, and it felt like she was a new girl at school rather than someone you'd known since your earliest memories. Over the past many months, you'd begun to forget her, and now she was back and her old name sounded strange and you noticed that, although you and all of your other friends had grown taller and rounder and prettier, somehow she had not.

She was always the littlest girl in your clique. A full head shorter than most everyone else, she acted funny and loud like the littlest girls sometimes did. Of all your friends, she was not the one it should have been. It should have been Mary Langan, who was busty and shy. Mary's mother was half gone whether she was on smack or off it, and most of the time they didn't seem to live anywhere. They sat on the side-walks with their stuff in boxes and old Sicilian men walked past, asking what was for sale. "Va'a farti friggere," you'd heard her mother say. *Get lost.* Then she'd add, "It's important we keep whatever we have." In their boxes, they had a cast-iron skillet, old shoes, and a wooden statue of a frog holding a doctor's bag. Mary's mother named him Henri Mancini. Mary called him Dr. Frog.

Or maybe it should have been Darla Santiago, whose father used to own a store before he died, but who now got evicted every month and went with her mother to the basement shelter at the Church of Christ. You used to go there too, before your mother went straight a year ago and began to sell Avon, and you remembered how it went. You remembered the lukewarm turkey slices, canned peas, and mashed potatoes made from powder. You remembered how the men and women all shared a single room at night, and how a man in the cot beside yours once said, "C'mon pretty girl, c'mon while your mama's not looking." Darla wouldn't have been able to say no or fake sleep. Darla, though proud, was not quick to do anything.

But the O Street Girl was quick and loud and her mother knew whole books by heart. Before she was the O Street Girl, she could imitate teachers and boys and rewrite love songs so that their lyrics described farting instead of romance. She said she was clever because her mother was smart. She said she was funny because her mom was nicer than yours. And you had your doubts only once, once when you went to her apartment and noticed a pile of shit on the floor. "It's from the dog," Beth said, and she cleaned it with newspaper. You didn't think she had a dog, but there was a leash in the corner, so you believed her as much as you worried for her. She said that her mother was nicer than yours, and in time you forgot the shit and the leash, and you believed her much more than you worried.

Then, one day last winter, the day after you walked home with her, arguing whether Harding was president before or after Coolidge, the day after she walked you to the door of your apartment building and said she'd see you tomorrow, you heard that she'd been found half-dead and bleeding on Oak Street. The papers called her the O Street Girl, but they gave her address so you knew who she was, and you read that her mother had thrown a party, and that Beth had been raped by some men there. Later, on the street, you heard that the men had paid, that it wasn't a rape but a sale, that Beth had been turning tricks, just like her mother did, just like your own mother did before going straight. Still later, in the papers again, you read that it was all her mother's idea, that her mother traded Beth's body for smack, and, for a minute, you wondered whether your friend had been tied up in that leash when the guests arrived that night. But there were men on the stoops who claimed to have been there, and who claimed that Beth had liked it. The final word on the street was that she liked it, and you decided to believe that.

One night ten years from now, when your kids are away at their father's and you can't sleep because of loneliness, you'll see a Girl X story on the news and remember Beth with a sudden, sharp ache, and the need to apologize will rise uncontrollably, like the need to profess a new love. You'll talk to national directory assistance until you find a number for an Elizabeth Dinard in Chicago, and when she answers her phone in a loud, whole voice, you'll forget what you meant to be sorry for.

"Who is this?" she'll ask, pretending. "I don't even know who you are." But she'll answer every question you should have asked but never did. She'll tell you that her mother and the men had gotten high, and that everyone, even her mother, kept laughing and laughing. She'll tell you that they pinned her down and that there was no place to look because every time she turned her head, she saw another man's naked flesh. She'll tell you that she closed her eyes, in an attempt to retreat within herself, but that retreat was impossible because the men took up every inch inside her, her rectum, vagina, mouth, even the air above her stomach. Their voices inhabited her ears. She'll tell you how one man laughed with pleasure when he said, "I forgot how it felt to fuck a tight cunt."

Back when she was the littlest girl in your clique, you all dragged old mattresses into the street on warm dry days, and used them as trampolines. You all could do flips on the mattresses as easily as you could sing or double-Dutch jump rope. Sometimes you all wrote, "We hex the Man" over and over on the laundromat wall. You got the idea of hexing from Nancy Drew. There was no such thing as best or worst, and to belong, you needed only to be there.

She was always the littlest girl in your clique, but now you and your friends had grown even taller, and she still had not grown, and the difference between you was even greater and made her look as strange as her old name sounded. She sat at her desk and did not talk to anyone. She looked down as if trying to hide, but she couldn't hide because she was responsible for the silence that surrounded her and filled the room. You considered waving hello to her, or at least talking to one of your other friends about the idea of waving hello to her, but no one was looking at anyone else and no one was talking, and you were fourteen years old and reluctant to be the first one to do anything. Then the second bell rang and Mr. Lloyd entered and he looked at the O Street Girl and said, "Oh. You're back. Good to see you. I didn't know that you were coming back." She didn't look up and she didn't talk and Jimmy Plato, who had three fingers on his left hand and had always been teased, started laughing.

On the phone ten years from now, she'll tell you how hard it was to come back to the same streets, the same school, to everyone thinking they knew what happened when no one knew what really happened. If she'd had money, she'll say, she would have had relatives in different cities. Or the relatives she did have would have taken her to someplace new. But starting fresh is a luxury, she'll tell you, and not everyone can.

Even though she lived with her grandmother now, even though her mother was in a mental institution for the year and some of the men were in jail, she was back in the same school, back with Jimmy Plato to whom Mr. Lloyd said nothing. Back with Mr. Lloyd, who was at least one hundred and eighty years old and who, because he had taught every grade level, had taught the O Street Girl three times before. To the O Street Girl, Mr. Lloyd said, "We're beginning now. Remove your cap."

She shook her head no. Of all your friends, she was not the one it should have been. Maybe it should have been you. Not now, of course, because your mother went straight. Not now, of course, because your mother served chicken that wasn't raw and pink the way it always was before she learned patience with things cooking. Now your mother even gave you flavored lipgloss from Avon. You wore bubble gum flavor when Neal Lenard first kissed you. He said that your lips tasted shiny.

"Remove your cap," Mr. Lloyd repeated. "There are no special privileges here."

Again she shook her head. And you began to think that perhaps you were wrong, that the O Street Girl in the papers was, in fact, someone else, and that this girl, your friend Beth, wasn't locked away in a hospital for broken bones and madness and bleeding, that she was hospitalized for cancer instead and, perhaps beneath her cap she was bald and ashamed. You had known two other children with cancer. They wore hats to school and then they stopped coming to school and then they were dead. Rosie was the first to die. You remembered the last time you saw her, how her mother carried her down the apartment stairs and into a taxi waiting by the curb. Rosie looked so shockingly small that you forgot to wave good-bye. And your mother, who had not yet gone straight, said, "Her mother's lucky. She'll get her life back." Now, of course, your mother cried whenever she thought about losing you, and claimed that something bad in the neighborhood's water poisoned children to death. And now you thought maybe there *was* something bad in the water, and maybe your friend was caught between being diagnosed and being dead.

But Mr. Lloyd walked to her desk and pulled off her cap, and she had as much hair as ever. It took you a minute to look lower than her hair, to notice that the top halves of her ears were missing. There were the lobes and the little holes she heard out of, but the seashell tops were gone and in their place were only curled, thick, red nubs. Jimmy Plato started laughing again, and then everyone laughed, and you laughed too because it was scary to see the strange curled stumps that used to be ears. Mr. Lloyd dropped the hat on the O Street Girl's desk and said, "No caps in class," but you could tell that he wished he'd never said anything.

On the phone ten years from now, she'll tell you how her mother pinched her ears until the cartilage tore, how the pain went down her throat and seemed to fill her eyes and lungs, how it seemed to coat the inside of her brain. She'll tell you that her mother did this to stop her from pleading, how her mother did this because she kept pleading with her to stop the men, her voice squeaky and desperate and implacable until her mother grabbed her ears and said, "Shut up goddammit or I'll rip them off!" She talked too much that night, she'll say, and a year passed before she could talk again.

But right now you didn't understand why the O Street Girl sat like a horrible doll, her head bowed and silent beneath her disgusting half-ears. It would have been easier if she had cried, if she had talked back as she once would have, if she had laughed with everyone else. Her silence made her ears all the more disgusting, and now you were terrified that she would look at you. You did not want to be looked at by a girl with hideous nubs for ears. You wanted to keep her far away from you, as if she embodied bad luck itself.

Jimmy Plato said, "Hey Ho Street, what happened to your ears?"

"That's enough," scolded Mr. Lloyd.

And everyone laughed again, and you laughed again too, and you knew that, from now on, she would be called Ho Street. And you hated her for her new nickname, and you hated her for her freak ears, and you hated her for what her mother and the men may have done, and because she may have liked it. A part of you remembered that she used to be your friend, but how much you used to like her did not erase how much you hated her now.

Mr. Lloyd yelled, "Shut up!" and you all stopped laughing, and Ho Street still didn't look up and she still didn't talk. And you knew that Jimmy Plato would no longer be the one to make fun of, that Ho Street's ears outdid his missing fingers. And you were glad that you did not wave hello when she first walked in, because that would have made you a target too, and you would have lost all your friends, and Neal Lenard would have told everyone that he'd only kissed you as a joke. Then everyone would have said that you'd gone further than you had, and they'd have jammed your locker with bubble gum. So you were glad that you did not say hello, and that she alone would be called a loser and a retard and a ho, and that no one—not even she—would expect you to be nice to her. She would know better than to approach you, and she would sit with the special ed kids at lunch knowing that no one at your table would make room for her. She would know better than to ask even you to scoot over on the slippery Formica cafeteria bench because, even though she'd become Ho Street, she knew the politics of childhood too.

On the telephone ten years from now, she'll tell you how men in her nightmares still call her Ho Street, even though as soon as she was old enough she fled to Chicago, hundreds of miles from anyone who'd ever called her that. She was already away in Chicago, her ears had been rebuilt by surgeons, and she thought she had a new start, when she heard that her mother had died. Her mother hadn't really died, though, not yet; it was just an act that time. But for a while she didn't know and, suddenly, she'll say, she wanted to turn tricks. She'll tell you how she quit her job, bought a pager, and met an old, married man in the Days Inn every afternoon. He liked for her to lie on her stomach while he covered her back and legs in massage oil—too much oil to ever wash off—and large, painful pimples took over her skin. She'll tell you that she made two hundred dollars a day, sometimes more, and only felt humiliated when her body came against her will. She'll tell you how, finally, she sold her pager and never went back. She'd never given him any way to track her down. He didn't even know her real name. She'll tell you, "That's how I really got over it. Not by starting fresh." And you will decide that she never got over it. For a moment you'll imagine inviting her to come live with you, to stay in your house until she really is whole, but you won't, because you won't want her body on your bedsheets or her ears on your pillows. Instead, you'll remember to say that you're sorry, and she'll reply, "What for?"

You'll say it wasn't that you didn't care. You'll say that sometimes, long ago, you'd even wished that she had died that night; you'd wished that dying could have saved her. You'll say, "I wished it for your sake," and she'll ask you, "Not for yours?"

She'll tell you, "I never once wished I was dead. Never once. Not even that first day back at school."

"Well I'm sorry," you'll repeat. "I'm sorry I didn't stand up for you."

"Look, I told you I don't even know who you are," she'll say. "I don't even remember which one you are."

Mr. Lloyd moved to the front of the room, lowered the map of the Western Hemisphere, pointed to Peru. "Eyes up here," he said. "Let's all focus on Peru." And his dusty voice mixed with the dusty light to lull you into private daydreams, in which neither Ho Street nor Peru had a place. You didn't wonder what she was thinking, or what she was wishing for. Instead you thought about Neal Lenard's slick tongue and how good it felt with his arms grabbing hard around your waist, in back of the basketball court, in the sweet dark cold of an early October night.

Leaving

The Chicago apartment had always been cold in the mornings, but it was colder now that Beth slept alone. Two weeks ago, Gina declared that sharing a bed was "too much togetherness" for her, and began sleeping on the floor in her study. They'd lived together for six months. Gina was thirty years Beth's elder, and while Beth's feelings vacillated between intense love and intense despair, Gina merely seemed to alternate between being able to tolerate Beth and not.

She squeezed the concentrate orange juice can, letting the frozen pulp thud into the pitcher. She licked the ice flecks from her fingers, started an egg frying. On the refrigerator hung a religious bookmark Beth's mother had once found in the street. The bookmark pictured two hugging bears and the whole text of I Corinthians 13 written out beneath the heading LOVE IS. Love is patient; that was listed first, but when Beth, in one of her despair spells, looked up the chapter in the library's King James, the words were different. "Love suffereth long," it read. *I suffer long*, she'd repeated. And she could feel herself changing, as if, at once, she was a woman on the American frontier shortly after the Civil War, stolid and unpresuming, birthing her own babies in the backs of carriages and reading the next day's weather in the stars.

The bookmark, now faded, had once been that shade of blue usually reserved for children's first-place sports awards. The hugging bears and textual letters were embossed in gold, and beneath the Bible excerpt read the announcement MAGGIE AND DAN, JUNE 13, 1987. Her mother had mocked it as she mocked all objects that referred to getting married with love and church services and party favors. Beth had mocked the bookmark with her mother, but it was the only one of her mother's possessions she took when she ran away at seventeen. As a child, she had secretly wanted to be married someday. Not the shack-up, beat-up, shoot-up common law deals her friends' mothers had. There was no such thing as common law anyway, not anymore. She wanted a wedding with crystal and registries and a cake with a statue of herself on top. Before she met Gina, she even thought she wanted a sleek man with features blank enough that it would seem he had no face at all. Now, at age twenty-one, she wanted to marry Gina.

When she heard Gina cough and rouse in the study, the muscles below Beth's shoulder blades tightened. She knew that she would not get what she wanted. For one thing, Gina claimed that even a marriage between women would be patriarchal and, for another thing, Gina didn't love her yet. Love was still possible, it seemed, perhaps, if Beth managed to do everything right. Gina stormed from the study to the bathroom, shut the door emphatically, and began a loud gargle. *I suffer long*, Beth thought as she slathered Gina's toast with boysenberry jam. It was the kind of food she had only recently begun to like. Before Gina, she'd been happy with any complete meal that came in a can. She remembered that Gina had once told her, "You're in a stage of emulation. Of wanting to be like me, of wanting to like what I like. Something else will come next."

You could love me next, Beth thought now, *or I could leave.* Maybe she would become that again: the kind of girl who leaves. Gina emerged from the bathroom, and each of her footsteps rendered Beth both happier and colder. She laid Gina's egg and toast on a plate and waited for her entrance.

"Morning." Gina kissed the back of her neck. A good day then. Beth exhaled, turned, threw her arms around Gina, and kissed her shoulder.

"Seven," Gina said. "You always give seven kisses."

She handed Gina the plate. "How did you sleep?"

"You know that woman who's subletting my apartment in San Francisco? I dreamed we were lovers."

"I don't like her."

Gina closed her eyes in strained patience. "Don't get threatened. I was just telling you my dream. How was your sleep?"

"It was all right."

"Good." Gina squatted down with her back against the wall and ate.

"I'm sorry."

"Stop apologizing. I thought you were going to stop with that."

"Yes." Beth poured a glass of orange juice and peered into the refrigerator. Suddenly, none of Gina's favorite foods appealed to her. "I don't live here," she said.

"What?"

"I don't feel as if I live here sometimes."

"Nor do I. Sometimes. Most of the time."

Downstairs, the neighbors began arguing. It was a mother and her teenage son, and it seemed they yelled constantly. Beth decided to make her own voice gentler. "Isn't the new sleeping arrangement helping you feel more at home?"

"It's helping some. We need to be more separate, Lizzie. More separate than we were."

She kept her head inside the refrigerator and thought, *Why? So you can have affairs?* But it didn't seem a long-suffering response. How could they become more separate? Lying beside Gina at night had been the singular closeness she had been able to depend on. She'd looked forward to it throughout the day, particularly when the weather was cold, looked forward to Gina's warmth and nearness that encroaching sleep muddled into a feeling almost like being loved.

"Jenny called," Beth muttered into the refrigerator. "She and her new girlfriend and I are going to Neighbors tonight for beers if you want to join us." She opened the crisper, picking through produce they'd bought a month ago and had soon forgotten. In one plastic bag, snow peas now swam in a thick, fetid, brown sap.

"I don't know. I need to get work done today and half the morning's going to be eaten up visiting my mother and waiting for the phone company to come install my line."

"You're getting your own phone line?"

"We talked about it. For my work. Remember?"

"I just thought, you know, since you're moving back home soon anyway, I mean, it just doesn't make that much sense to do all that for a month or two."

"They'll turn it off when I leave. You won't be stuck paying for it, if that's your concern."

"No, that wasn't what I was thinking."

"It's just a phone line, Lizzie."

"I just don't understand why you need your own phone and your own bed if we're supposed to be a couple." Blue and white fur checkered the ancient salsa in a jar.

"We are a couple, Lizzie! It's just that I need my space too."

"But you'll have lots of space coming up! When you move back to San Francisco."

"Come out of the fridge, Lizzie. I'm not leaving for another two months."

Beth held the mold-filled jar of salsa in one hand, stood straight, stared at Gina, wanted to hurl it at the wall behind her head, or maybe even at the head itself.

"You let that girl in here while I'm at work, I'll kill you," the mother downstairs shouted.

Instantly, Beth remembered her own mother's yelling face and threatening eyes. With excessive gentleness, she placed the jar of salsa into the garbage can. "I wonder where that woman works," she said.

"Probably at a cocktail bar." Gina finished her breakfast and brought the plate to the sink.

"Not all single mothers work as cocktail waitresses, you know. Mine didn't."

"Yes, I know. Yours didn't work at all."

"She was sixteen!" Beth began her standard mother defense, but stopped because she noticed Gina laughing. "I have to get ready for work," she sighed.

"I was just teasing," Gina said.

"Well, it's not a nice thing to tease about. Besides, at least I had the decency to take care of my mother."

"Before you ran away," Gina said. Then she sighed, "I take care of mine too. That's what I'm doing."

"Yes, for another two whole months. I'm perfectly aware of that."

"Lizzie, I can't manage all my problems and your fragility too."

"I have to be at work in an hour."

"I'm not going to take it on. Not today."

"Fine. Don't." In the bathroom mirror, Beth noticed red scales on her neck, a thin galaxy of hives trailing from her ear to her shoulder. *Only serves to make me uglier*, she thought. She knew that appearances shouldn't matter to her, and that they didn't matter to Gina. Still, she'd always hoped to grow into beauty someday. Now she could see herself beginning to age, but beauty had still not come. At twenty-one, her face was still childlike and naive-looking beneath her already-graying, frizzy hair, but already her eyes looked dull, and her crooked, crowded teeth seemed to be growing yellow.

By the time she got out of the bathroom, Gina was gone. In the foyer of her building, the hobbled old superintendent caulked a new mailbox onto the wall.

"Are we getting new mailboxes, Mr. Kelley?"

The old man didn't answer, but Beth noticed that the new mailbox had Gina's name on it, and that the label on the box they used to share had been replaced and now only had Beth's name. "My roommate got her own mailbox, Mr. Kelley?" She always referred to Gina as her roommate when talking to Mr. Kelley.

"Yep," the man said, smiling cheerfully. "She bought it yesterday, asked if she could hang it up. Said I'd do it for her."

"What does she need her own box for?"

"Said you gals get a lot of mail. Too much for one box. Keep warm out there, honey. It's frigid. You got a scarf?"

"Yes, sir." Outside, the snow had been ploughed into knee-high drifts. It leaked through Beth's pants and filled her shoes. She would take the train to work today. Her ratty car wouldn't consent to starting in this cold and, besides, it would take too long to dig out of its parking space along the curb. And if she dug out her own car, she wouldn't be able to just drive away without digging out Gina's. She couldn't imagine leaving Gina to heave all those heavy shovels full of snow herself. She decided to shovel out both cars later.

An hour later, sitting in the conference room with melting snow forming a puddle beneath her feet, Beth pushed her coffee to the edge of the table and watched her supervisor pass the next database assignment around. Beside her, Jenny Frye whispered, "Is Gina coming to Neighbors?"

"Maybe. She's not sure. I can't wait to meet Dana."

"You'll love her."

Beth nodded, bitterly anticipating how much she'd like Dana, whom Jenny met less than a month ago, but who already couldn't bear to spend an evening or a night away from her, who took baths with her and sucked her toes. Jenny had told her all of that. And Beth had masked her envy with a feigned girlish enthusiasm she'd forgotten how to feel, though she'd felt it about Gina when they'd first met, not very long before. Jenny's world of beery kisses and newly realized lesbians desperately, passionately in love, was not Beth's. Its entrance belonged to girls who, even though they were Beth's age, now seemed so much younger they made no sense to her. When Beth talked to her breathless, happy friends, she sometimes saw her own words suspended over her head, as if she were assuming a role in a comic strip.

She knew that Gina wouldn't join her. "I got tired of that scene twenty years ago," she always said. "Those little girls exhaust me." But something always exhausted Gina, it seemed, and, for some reason, this made Beth feel tender toward her, as if Gina had been born with a weak constitution, or was a small, long-ago woman with consumption whose energy needed to be conserved. Sometimes, when Gina came unexpectedly into her room to kiss her goodnight and said, with an almost childish coyness, "You love me, don't you?" Beth imagined that if she could love her more than she'd ever previously been loved, loyalty alone would win Gina over to reciprocity. But she also suspected that it wouldn't work. Often, when Gina talked about her less spectacular former lovers, she referred to them with epithets: "The Lunatic" and "The Bore." Beth worried that she would be named someday too.

As her boss at the head of the conference table began to rattle on about their new client's needs, Beth thought how odd it was to be tied to the railroad tracks like this, to be paralyzed in the face of oncoming devastation. The old woman said, "So to frame it one way, the reason we have corporate domination is what? The goods, yes? The stronger company has the goods that the weaker wants. Coarse parlance, perhaps, but there's your unmistakable strategy."

On her notepad, Beth wrote, "What are Gina's goods, then? I am the weaker. What goods does she have that I want?" She didn't know.

Gina left the house before eight thirty. Moving into the study was the best thing she'd done in months. Lizzie was infuriating to sleep with, restless and clingy as a toddler. Every day, Gina had woken up anxious and exhausted. But now, here she was, out in the early morning's abrasive cold, feeling alert and clean.

When she was alone, outside, moving, Gina felt all right. It even seemed, at those times, that she had an inviolate kernel of innate happiness, the happiness she remembered having as a child, in the rare moments her mother wasn't blaring at her: that normal, childlike feeling of self-love and a confident, petty triumph, like Bugs Bunny's. Walking alone now through the bracing cold, she felt as if great things awaited her, and that greatness could be waiting around any corner. She thought of her career: lucky, so far, but not lucrative. She'd been widely published in the better political science journals, and was now living off a grant that was the envy of talking heads everywhere.

Gina saw herself as if from above and compared her mind and its accomplishments, absurdly, to Lizzie's. Thinking of their connection pierced sharply through Gina's happiness, yet she couldn't stop; she kept Lizzie's face in mind almost against her will. She and Lizzie

were so unequal, and their inequality—which, in Gina's mind, evoked
the image of a child measuring her small hands against her mother's—
was made cloying by tenderness rather than mitigated by it. Lizzie
was a computer geek, or at least that was what Lizzie called herself.
Really, she was only a glorified secretary with a lucky knack for com-
puters despite a substandard education, which included no college at
all. It was a mediocre occupation; a mediocrity, Gina often thought,
that seemed to suit Lizzie and all her little friends. Gina knew that
Lizzie would never get anywhere in this life. She'd be lucky to even
gain grudging promotions into a job that included an office rather
than a cubicle. Gina herself had a Ph.D. from the University of Chicago.
Her dissertation focused on game theory, something Lizzie had never
even heard of before Gina tried to explain it to her.

Gina stopped at a coffee shop. Inside, it smelled of skin that
had been sweating beneath winter coats—a close, humid, thick smell
that soured what little remained of her happiness. As she did every
day, Gina bought a latte for herself and a hot cocoa to bring to her
mother. She dreaded, as she did every day, the impending visit, and
her mother's insistences about who Gina really was and what she
really wanted. *The problem*, Gina decided, *is that Mother's opinions
always sound at least partly credible, and her claim to have all the answers
is, well, seductive.* How easy Gina's life might be if she obeyed.
Walking—more slowly now—from the coffee shop to her mother's
apartment, Gina glanced at her reflection in the silvery glass of an
office building. She was—inconceivably, it seemed—middle-aged,
carrying two cardboard cups and taking care to avoid slipping on
the patches of salt-resistant ice on the sidewalks. Her jeans, she
noticed, were the style only middle-aged women might wear. Lizzie,
for example—and even the girl's name made her chest and shoulders feel burdened—would look ridiculous, prematurely sedate and
stale, in jeans like these. She hadn't noticed, when she'd bought the
pants, how much her taste had aged, and this startled and depressed
her. *Greatness will not come*, Gina decided brutally. *It won't come to
me any more than it will come to Lizzie.*

Gina had met Lizzie at a bad moment. She'd gotten this grant only a week before her mother, at age seventy-five, had her second stroke. Gina's mother demanded—as the grant was for two years and, as "writing and research could be done anywhere"—that Gina leave San Francisco to spend time in Chicago with her, during these, her "September days." Gina flew home to her mother's side at once. She started doing her research at the University of Chicago library, and on a rainy day, spotted a sopping wet Lizzie thumbing through a book of case studies on homeless mothers. Lizzie stared relentlessly at her, smiled. Her dark bangs and open-faced sweetness peaked Gina's curiosity. It had been a long time since someone that much younger had flirted with her.

"You're a sociologist?" Gina had asked.

"No," Lizzie answered, laughing. With her eyes, she indicated the book she held. "I'm just reading this for fun."

"Looks like fun," Gina joked, and Lizzie laughed again. Gina didn't know that Lizzie never ordinarily went to the U of C library, or that Lizzie belonged at the U of C about as much as a hamster would have. Six months before, Lizzie had gone to the hospital nearby to have surgery on her ears—they'd been damaged in some freak accident Lizzie refused to talk about—and she'd come, that day, for a follow-up appointment. She'd only gone to the library to pass the time and get out of the rain. But Gina didn't know any of this, and instead imagined that Lizzie was a precocious doctoral candidate, one of those gifted young lesbian academics. She thought of the ex-girlfriend who'd just broken up with her in San Francisco, a brilliant performance artist who'd said that she wasn't attracted to Gina because, to her, intelligence wasn't "as erotic as youth." The performance artist wasn't even that young; she was in her thirties, and Gina imagined being able to tell her, victoriously, about Lizzie. By the time she found out that Lizzie was neither a brilliant academic nor a lesbian in any experienced sense of the word, it was too late. Lizzie had already grasped onto her so tightly that Gina felt unable to extricate herself without shattering Lizzie's neophyte office-girl heart.

Gina's mother lived in the Senior Plaza, a two-tower apartment building designed to accommodate one's progressive skid into dehabilitation. Tower A, her mother's tower, contained ordinary apartments occupied by elderly people who lived "unassisted" and a dormitory-like dining hall where the tower tenants convened at set times for meals. Tower B, into which many of the current Tower A residents would ultimately move, contained two-person hospital rooms, call buttons, and nurses who brought bedpans and trays of pureed food.

The two towers shared a lobby, and Gina waved to the doorman who was chatting with a Tower B tenant seated beside the front desk in her wheelchair and house slippers, plastic tubes up her nose.

Her mother's apartment was close to the lobby on the ground floor, as the stroke had left her unable to comfortably walk to the elevators at the end of the hall. She answered the door before Gina knocked. "Hello, sweet." She kissed Gina on both cheeks.

"I brought your cocoa." Gina gave her arm to her mother to lean on and helped her across the plush red carpet to the springy black leather sofa. Gina placed the cardboard cups on coasters atop the glass coffee table and sat down.

"Your scalp is so chapped," Gina's mother said, not yet seated, her eyes above the level of Gina's head, and her fingers on Gina's skin. "You're not used to the cold anymore. It's chapping straight through your hair."

"I always forget to wear a hat," Gina said, pulling away. "Sit down, Mother."

"Hang on." Her mother began a slow trek toward the hallway. "I've got something for that."

"It's all right, Mother. Sit down. I can get my own hat."

"Just wait. It's not a hat."

"I'll help you." Gina stood.

"Sit down. I'm no invalid."

Gina gazed into the large mirror on the wall opposite the sofa. Amazingly, she looked younger here than she had on the street; she wore an almost adolescent expression of defiant impatience.

Her mother, Gina decided, made her own identity, her own situation in time, slippery. She pushed her hair from her forehead and tried to gauge whether her skin was truly chapped. On either side of the mirror, old photographs of her mother's Chicago theater days hung in brass frames. She'd never gotten beyond Chicago productions, allegedly because, even though she could "act circles around everyone," she'd "never had the kind of figure they want in New York."

"Polysorbate 80!" Gina's mother brought a small medicinal-looking tube over to the couch. "Here, sit on the floor in front of me, and I'll rub it into your head."

"I don't need it, Mother. I just need to wear a hat when it's cold."

"You don't want to damage your scalp. What if your hair started to fall out? It's in our family, you know. Your grandma was bald as an egg when she died. Now sit down."

Gina sighed then sat on the floor, her head tilted back against her mother's knees. Again, time and place slipped away, and she was a child, her mother's industrious fingers preparing her hair for some event: some performance of her mother's, perhaps, that Gina would be made to watch from backstage. And, just as she had felt as a child, Gina knew that her mother would eventually pull her fingers away and survey her with disappointment. Suddenly afraid, Gina wanted to cry or slap her mother's hand. *Calm down*, she told herself. *She's an old woman now. And you'll miss her when...* But she wasn't certain she would. "How are you feeling today, Mother?"

"Same as yesterday," her mother said. Thick, cold goop saturated the roots of Gina's hair. "Can't complain."

For weeks, she had been afraid to say it, but now she did. "I'm going to go back home soon, now that you're up and about again."

"Home? You just got here!"

"You'll be okay now."

"I'll be so lonely, Gina."

"I'm sorry." Gina looked down at her hands. She could imagine her mother and Lizzie crying together, angry at her for not being the good daughter or the devoted lover. *But I try,* Gina told herself; *in my own way I really do try.* She had always wanted, simply, to maintain some kind of integrity, some kind of wholeness; she hadn't wanted to damage anyone in the process.

Her mother's pudgy fingers stood still on Gina's head. "I was so happy when you got here, when you met that girlfriend of yours. I've seen her look at you, Gina. She's crazy about you. Why are you running away?"

Gina imagined Lizzie's little worshipful face, her startled-looking, almost madly wide eyes, and shuddered. "I'm in over my head with Lizzie, Mother. She's a little girl. I don't know how to end it unless I leave." *I'm in over my head with you too,* she wanted to say, but she kept the blame on Lizzie. *Lizzie the Scapegoat,* Gina thought. *Ah well, Lizzie wouldn't mind; she'd lay her head on the block gladly, saying, "I love you, I love you, I'd do anything for you."* Lizzie professed her love so often, so expectantly, that being loved now felt odious to Gina. She told her mother, "I don't love Lizzie." But it didn't sound truthful, so she qualified it. "Not enough anyhow."

Her mother took a theatrical breath. "You know what your problem is?" And, as always when her mother got ready to make a pronouncement, Gina felt a surge of hope: the hope that this time, perhaps, she would be understood; the hope that her mother could, in fact, make sense of the parts of her she herself could not. "You can't love anyone who makes herself available to you."

"Oh, Mother," Gina sighed, disappointed again. "That's everybody's problem."

"Still." Her mother quickly donned the scheming voice she'd used, forty-five years ago, to cajole Gina into "sitting and reading like a good quiet mouse" at her mother's rehearsals. "It's a shame to leave her for someone else to snatch up. She must be a hot potato in the sack, a young thing like that."

"Mother!" But imagining Lizzie with someone else, giving looks and kisses to someone else, made Gina's stomach ache. "I don't want to talk about that, Mother. It's private."

"You know, most people would be grateful to have such a liberal mother. Roberta Foxx, upstairs? Her son Barry's gay, and she hasn't talked to him about sex in twenty years."

"Perhaps the two of you can trade progeny, then."

"Oh you." She withdrew her hands from Gina's head and wrapped them around her shoulders, Polysorbate 80 sticking to Gina's sweater. "Your visits are the only joy I have." She kissed Gina's earlobe noisily.

"My god, what's in that stuff?" Gina removed her mother's hands from her clothes and pulled her head away from her mother's mouth. "Petroleum jelly?"

"See?" her mother said, her face against Gina's neck. "Look how you pull away from love."

"That's not it!"

Her mother looked at her, and Gina was surprised by the fear in her old-lady eyes. "You don't want to grow old alone," she said. "Stay in Chicago. Hang on to that little girlfriend. You're too much in your head all the time, too all alone in there. I'm telling you, Gina, mothers know about these things. We're always right."

On her lunch break, Beth took a walk through the snow to the public university campus near her office and watched the undergraduate couples walking, laughing, hand in hand. *They breathe a different kind of air*, Beth told herself, and imagined that they all slept in sex-sweated sheets every night, their limbs knotted helplessly together as if to save one another from drowning. Thoughts of her own stoic bed sheets and their almost prudish detachment from carnality made her insides feel ash-covered and sour. *I am dying*, she told herself. Then, walking behind one couple, she heard the boy tell the girl, "Man, we gotta start going to class," before he laughed, pushed the hair from the girl's eyes, and kissed her hotly on the mouth. *I am dying*, Beth repeated, *but at least I get my work done.* The boy looked at her, noticed that she'd been staring at them kiss, and laughed as if etiquette required him to feel an embarrassment he couldn't muster.

"Sorry," Beth said, and edged past them. Gina had never kissed her like that.

After work, Beth didn't necessarily want to go to Neighbors, but the prospect of going home to be ignored seemed worse than the prospect of being bored in a bar. She spotted Jenny, who waved, and another woman who didn't work at their office. She was beautiful, with a small, intelligent face. She looked to be about thirty years old. *Dana*, Beth thought miserably.

"This is Dana!" Jenny said, but she pushed a different woman up from her barstool toward Beth. The mythical Dana. She was not what Beth had expected. Except in terms of her own lack, beauty meant almost nothing to her, and she felt no differently, usually, about the ugly. But Dana, the mythical Dana, was astonishingly ugly, an ugliness that could not be ignored or looked past because it seemed to have an odor and color all its own. It wasn't that she was marked with any obvious defect. In isolation, her features were benign enough, but added together, somehow, they seemed both flaccid and filled with an aggressive and toxic ooze. She stared at Beth for too long, she stared at Beth's *breasts* for too long, and she let her mouth hang open about an eighth of an inch for no reason. Her lips looked wet. "Good to meet you, Liz," she said flatly.

There were no empty stools at the table, so Jenny scooted over, allowing a crescent of space on which Beth, presumably, could sit.

"I'll stand, thanks." She wondered why the mythical Dana, whom Jenny had once called "the epitome of courtesy" hadn't offered her seat.

"Hey Jen, get me another Miller, couldya?" Dana asked.

"Sure, sweetie." She kissed Dana on the mouth before standing, wallet in hand.

"Trouble at home?" Dana asked.

"No," Beth said shortly before looking at the other woman, the beautiful stranger. "Do you know these guys?"

"No," the stranger said. "I teach at the college. This is the only bar around here where the students don't go."

Dana stroked Beth's fingertips, bringing her attention back.

"Why are your eyes so sad?" Her look mixed sympathy with heavy-handed flirtation.

"They're not!" Beth pulled her hand away. "Jesus, Dana. If someone you just met tells you there's nothing wrong, don't assume you know better."

"It's just a vibe, Liz. I just get the saddest vibe from you."

"I don't believe in vibes," she said, but she tried to put some cheer into her eyes anyway. "I'm going to get a beer," she told the beautiful stranger. "Would you like one?"

"All right," the stranger said. Then she added, "Rachel. I'm Rachel."

"I'm Liz," Beth said stupidly.

"I know," Rachel answered. "Liz who's having trouble at home."

"I'm not, really."

"What's her name?" Rachel asked. "The one who's giving you trouble."

"Gina," Beth answered.

She bought three beers, one for Rachel and two for herself, which was more than enough for her on an empty stomach, and she drank the first one standing at the bar. Soon Gina would be gone, and her life would be gutted out and in need of filling. She imagined the transparent, hard shell of her life being filled with databases and memos and beer. She began on the second bottle and bought a third. By the time she returned to the table, she was drunk.

"So it was a huge snowdrift," Jenny was saying. "There I was, just me and this little old lady who was walking her dog, and I'm pushing the car and she's steering and the dog's on the sidewalk barking his head off."

"You drove in the snow?" Beth asked.

"Yeah. My car too," Dana added with gruff petulance.

"You let her drive in the snow?"

"It was really okay." Jenny smiled. "She's from North Carolina. She has no idea how to drive in this kind of weather, and I had to go to work, so she let me take her car."

"And she got it stuck in the middle of the damn street," Dana huffed.

"Why didn't you go with her? Why weren't you there to help her?"

"Calm down, Liz." Now Rachel's hand was atop hers. Later, she would tell Beth that she worked as a professor and that, even though Beth was younger than many of her students, she would really like it if Beth were to call sometime. And Beth would keep the number in her wallet for weeks and think about calling more often than she should have. And eventually, before Gina left, Beth would call Rachel, and Rachel would sound glad to hear her voice. Just then, however, Beth felt a surge of anger as Rachel announced, as if addressing a lecture hall, "She and Gina are having trouble."

"We are not having trouble!" Beth was sobbing like an imbecile. "But if Gina's car was stuck in the snow, I'd never make her get it out herself. I'd be on a train in a minute to get to her to help her. That's what you do when you care about someone. It's just basic."

Gina could hear the neighbors fighting again. She was instantly flooded with homesickness, for her books and her old apartment, for her downstairs neighbor who talked too loudly and her upstairs neighbor who exercised through the night on a motorized treadmill, creating a thunderous whir. Those things had annoyed Gina when she'd lived in San Francisco, but now they seemed unsung comforts, the familiar noises of a life that was really her own.

"I should just kill myself!" the teenager downstairs said with the expected level of teenage angst.

"Will you shut up?" the mother droned. Probably a drunkard, Gina thought. What types. Both of them. There will be punches thrown next, and crying.

"What the fuck did you think you were doing with her in my house? I specifically warned you not to have her in here when I was out," the mother's voice croaked.

"At least she loves me," the teenager hollered, continuing the script.

Gina ferreted through one of the boxes she'd never bothered unpacking and found some cotton to use as earplugs. She opened the San Francisco newspaper the subletter had sent in her weekly packet of unforwarded mail. She glanced through the apartment listings and was glad she'd chosen to sublet rather than letting her lease go; the rents had soared even higher since she was last there. She felt sorry for the subletter; she would never be able to find anything affordable. Last night, in Gina's dream, the subletter's bare skin was inhumanly silver, with a hairless, glasslike smoothness, an almost molten perfection. Gina had woken up before she'd had a chance to touch her. *If Lizzie could just be like that*, she thought. Then she stopped herself. Nobody was like that. Still, if Lizzie could be a little more distant, a little more dignified; if Gina felt, every now and then, that Lizzie's love was something she'd earned and had to work to keep.

"You want me to leave?" the teenager shouted, the words loud enough to burrow through Gina's cotton earplugs. "Fine! I do everything around here. Let's see how you do without me."

Lizzie's bedroom had the only windows that faced the building's front entrance, and Gina looked out one of them to see if, this time, the boy was really going. The room smelled soft, like Lizzie. *If only*, Gina thought, *if only...* She thought of the telephone man's quizzical look when she'd told him the line would only operate until she left in a month or two. She thought of her mother who, upon hearing Gina's plans to get the phone line installed, had said, "It sounds to me as if you don't really want to go back home, as you call it, at all."

She pressed her nose to the glass and peered out into the night. The teenager's angular body strutted across the street, past someone who was using a shovel to clear the snow away from a car parked at the curb. Finally, the boy walked out of Gina's range of vision, presumably through the snowy streets to the safety of his little girlfriend's warm arms. Gina thought of Lizzie's warm, vulnerable body and involuntarily imagined it pressed against some other woman's, or maybe even some man's. The thought made her throat close with confusion and jealousy and longing. *If only...* Her mother was right, perhaps. Maybe she did want to stay. The figure with the shovel moved to a second car and began clearing the snow away from that one too. Through the heating vent came sounds from the downstairs apartment; Gina could hear the boy's mother sobbing. You don't want to grow old alone, Gina's poor, frightened mother had said. Outside, the shoveler moved to yet another car.

Gina returned to the living room and resumed reading. What if Lizzie was the last girl to come along? What if Gina found herself alone in twenty years, like her mother was? Maybe, she decided, her feelings for Lizzie were small simply because the girl was too available. Maybe that was all love was, a jockeying for position, something you could only feel when you had to strive for it. What if Gina could become the one who loved, and Lizzie could become the one who asked for distance and backed away? Then Gina would have the opportunity to stoke her attachment to Lizzie with the delicious longings and perils of the chase. *When Lizzie gets home tonight*, Gina promised herself, *I'll take Lizzie in my arms, and try, really try to invert this, this... thing we have.* She made it through the entire San Francisco newspaper before she heard the front door unlock. But as Lizzie's footsteps came nearer up the stairs, Gina felt more and more nervous, suffocated. If only Lizzie would help to flip it all around. If only she would arrive slightly different, older, more in control. She looked up, hoping. Lizzie's nose was red and running.

"You're still awake," Lizzie said, smiling as if staying awake were an accomplishment. Gina felt disgust cauterize her hopes.

"Did you have a nice evening with your chums?"

"I met that girl Jenny's so crazy about. What's all over your hair?"

"Some stuff my mother put on it. What's Jenny's friend like?"

"Bossy and slothful. I'll shampoo your hair out in the sink later, if you want."

"I'm not a child," Gina snapped.

"I know." Lizzie wiped her nose on her coat sleeve. She disappeared into the kitchen, and Gina could hear her fill the tea kettle. She braced herself; soon Lizzie would be offering tea, cookies, and favors. But instead she stood in the doorway, leaned against the wall and asked, "If I didn't have a car, would you let me drive yours in a blizzard, or would you drive me yourself?"

Maybe, Gina thought, *this is the kind of change I'm looking for; riddles beat abject servitude. Tests, after all, can be failed.* Gina tried to figure out the implications of both answers. To let her drive in a blizzard would be uncaring, certainly, a laissez-faire attitude that might have suited a more independent or stubborn woman, but not Lizzie. But to say that she would drive her herself would mean that she didn't trust Lizzie's competence, that she didn't respect her autonomy. "I would give you cab fare," she answered.

Lizzie sighed, blew into her hands, rubbed them together, and held them to her earlobes. Suddenly Gina understood; the servitude had already happened and this riddle was somehow connected to it. "Was that you outside just now, digging the snow away from cars?" Gina asked.

Lizzie smiled her little girl smile. "You're like my mother, you know," she said. "My mother loved so many other people. Men. Just not me. That was her power over me, her ability to love. It's the same with you."

"Lizzie. Was that you digging out every damn car on the block?"

"I've been acting like such a baby," Lizzie continued, ignoring the question, ignoring her lunatic doormat behavior of digging out an entire city street's worth of cars. "I've been waiting for you to love me, when you never will. You'll give me cab fare, that's what you said."

"You!" Gina hollered, but had no idea what to say next. She wanted to rage, *How the hell am I supposed to love you? You have no self-respect! You have no idea how to jockey for position. Who could love someone like you?* But she didn't want to see Lizzie cry. *Yes, Mother,* she thought, *I can't love anyone who's available. But neither can Lizzie, and neither can you. That's why you both love me. I'm the object of your suffering, and both of you like it that way.*

It was better, Gina decided, to live alone inside one's own head. She closed her eyes; whatever she had might not be genius or the path to greatness, but her thoughts were clean and sharp and she owned them entirely. She took a deep breath and spoke quietly to Lizzie. "You, with your petty understanding of power dynamics and reductive notions of filial relationships, may not give me some absurd driving-in-snow litmus test to signify all the ways in which I'm deficient. It doesn't work that way. Grow up."

The kettle whistled on the burner, and Lizzie disappeared from the kitchen doorway. The noise stopped. "The plough blocked all the cars in with snow," she said. "There could be an emergency. Someone might need to leave fast."

Afterbirth

Beth opened her eyes and read midnight on the green digital alarm clock numbers.

"The baby, Beth, can't you hear her?" her mother had just said in Beth's dream.

Kerry offered a sustained squawk from her crib across the room. "I hear her," Beth said to the empty space her mother did not occupy now that she was awake. Her nerves jangling, she fumbled out of bed, groped to the crib, picked up the yelling Kerry, and lugged her out into the living room. She didn't take the time to turn on the living room lights before settling down on the couch with the screaming infant, lifting her T-shirt and attaching Kerry to her left breast. The noise stopped as she felt Kerry root and Beth's heartbeat slowed to a more regular pace.

Her eyes adjusted to the dark by the time she recognized the scraping-bottom feeling of her left breast draining. She surveyed her milk supply—her left breast looked floppy and shriveled; the right looked enormous and dense. She switched Kerry to her right breast and watched it deflate. There were spots of milk on Kerry's cheek, and more dribbled out the side of her mouth as she fell asleep. When Kerry stopped sucking altogether, Beth pulled her nipple away and stood, her head spinning and her teeth aching as if they were rotting away at the roots. When the dizziness abated enough for her to walk, she hauled Kerry back to her crib and plunked her down on her back. She lay alone in her own bed, her T-shirt sticking to her where milk splotches made it wet. She imagined that one of her mother's small, cool hands had found its way onto her shoulder and stayed there.

Beth looked at the green numbers on the alarm clock. She'd managed to sleep forty-five minutes since the last time the baby had cried.

"I've got her." She stood and bumbled her way back to the crib. Kerry, an infuriatingly helpless animal, lay flailing and screaming. Beth slung her over one shoulder, jostled her up and down and hoped a burp would cure her. But Kerry was smacking her lips together so she trudged back to the couch, turned the light on to wake herself up, and lifted her T-shirt. She couldn't remember the percentage of water in the human body even though she was only twenty-three and had learned it in high school, but as she gushed milk into Kerry's mouth, she wondered if the percentage of water in her own body had sailed way above the norm in the past three weeks since Kerry was born and her milk had come. She remembered the old idea of the four humors that her mother talked about sometimes while reciting Shakespeare. Beth wondered why water wasn't on that list, and if the excess water in her body could make her sick. *It's good that I have Kerry then*, Beth told herself; *she's leeching me*. After a few minutes, Kerry's eyes closed and the pattern of her sucking slowed. Beth pulled her nipple away, hoping Kerry was asleep. The baby hollered.

Beth stuffed her breast back into Kerry's mouth. She leaned her head against the back of the couch and rested her feet on the coffee table. In the street four stories below her Chicago apartment, a car alarm sounded—the kind that alternately hooted and buzzed. No one turned the alarm off and Beth closed her eyes, hoping to stave off a headache. She woke when Kerry fell asleep and detached from her, her head falling heavy against her lap. She carted Kerry back to the crib, laid her on her back and dropped into bed, leaving the living room lights on for later.

Beth was dreaming again the next time Kerry cried. She didn't remember the dream, exactly, but felt its afterimage—her mother's arms in dark cloth, silky and warm, encasing her as they never really had. Back on the couch with Kerry, Beth felt confused and far away, put her body on autopilot, fed the baby. She occupied the junction between sleeping and not—simultaneously felt Kerry nursing and heard her own snoring. She closed her eyes, enjoyed the phantom feeling of the dark embrace again. She waited for Kerry to sleep and longed for her own mother, for that quiet, dark warmth all to herself. When Kerry stopped eating, she opened her eyes wide and screeched loudly enough to disabuse Beth of her fantasies. Her teeth hurt.

Beth threw Kerry over one shoulder and whacked her back until she burped. Her butt was close enough to Beth's head for Beth to be able to smell that Kerry needed changing, but the walk from the couch to the changing table seemed incomprehensibly far. She imagined it would help if she could just be with that warmth a minute or two first, so she held Kerry in burping position awhile longer, closed her eyes, and let Kerry's cries and the ghost of her dream blend together. It was almost bearable. It dulled the noise just enough.

"BETH!" She startled awake, imagined her mother standing next to the couch, yelling her name. Then she heard Kerry, whose chin remained on her shoulder, still crying. She didn't know how much time had passed.

"Sorry," she said, and carried Kerry to the changing table. She took off Kerry's dirty diaper and daubed her bottom with a pre-wet cloth.

"Jesus, if you can't even take care of a baby, Beth!" she imagined her mother might say.

"Then?" Beth asked. She powdered Kerry and put a new diaper on her bottom. "If I can't take care of a baby, then *what?*"

She didn't know how her mother would respond.

Three weeks earlier, Beth was discharged from the hospital only twelve hours after Kerry's birth. A year before, her mother had faked her own death and Beth, propelled strangely by angry grief, had quit her decent job, left her decent lover, Rachel, and moved out of her decent apartment. Then she'd gotten hired by an older, married john with whom she spent afternoons at the Days Inn. She hadn't expected to get pregnant, but once it happened it seemed a preinscribed course, the only outcome she'd never wanted for her life and, therefore, the only outcome that had ever been possible. Her own mother had been a single mother, and Beth had always wanted to leave their shameful poverty behind. But at twenty-three, single and pregnant herself, she had no health insurance and no job. Initially, she didn't know what she'd do for money, but she soon found a job conducting telephone surveys from her home and a hospital that allowed uninsured women to pay a flat fee for prenatal care and a normal delivery with no overnight post-partum stay.

Her job paid poorly. If she managed, somehow, to refrain from lending any money to her not-dead mother, she would have just enough to pay the hospital bill, rent and utilities, with twenty-five dollars a week left over to spend on food and, after the baby came, diapers. She contacted Public Aid and WIC, but her salary was too high for her to qualify for any assistance. When she was small, she'd once asked her mother why she didn't work at any jobs other than selling sex. Her mother had answered, "Because we'd be even poorer if I had a job the government liked."

Beth was on the telephone, asking survey questions, when her labor started. She finished the survey, called her doctor, told him about the contractions and said she was pretty sure. "Pretty sure isn't good enough," he'd answered. "Labor is like love. If you're not a hundred percent certain, it's not it." She thought briefly, hungrily of Rachel. She had loved Rachel, certainly. What she felt now, therefore, could not have been labor.

That night, she cooked spaghetti but her stomach hurt too badly to eat. She made a plate for later, covered it in Saran wrap and put it in the refrigerator. Then she tried sitting on the couch to watch a basketball game, but couldn't get comfortable. She moved from the couch to the rocking chair and finally discovered she was only comfortable sitting on the toilet—with the seat cover up and her skirt and panties still on. She held a wristwatch in one hand and timed the pains. "Hard, regular contractions," her doctor had said. "Call back when you have hard, regular contractions." She waited. She'd left the television on and could hear the game; she heard the first and second quarters, the half-time interviews, the third and fourth quarters, the post-game show. Throughout, she timed the pains. Five minutes, three minutes, six minutes, two minutes. "Hard and regular," the doctor had said. Did "regular" mean contractions of equal length? Whenever she tried to stand up, the pain prevented her. She wanted to split herself apart and let some of the pieces run free, imagined shards of herself running hard and fast in the cold of a winter night, yelling at the top of their lungs.

The nighttime news began then ended, and a row of late-night comedy talk shows played. Beth hated the grating sound of audience laughter, but when she stood, intending to turn off the television, her stomach churned mercilessly. She managed to retreat back to the toilet. Her stomach felt calmer after she'd thrown up, and Beth wondered if she was mistaking some sort of virus for early labor. She decided to go to bed, but as soon as she lay down the pain started again, propelled her back to the toilet where she sat, watching the wristwatch and waiting.

A more ferocious pain mounted her. Loud and dull, it sat on her lower back for a moment before burrowing its way though her internal organs, down her appendages, into her fingers and toes. It occupied every inch of her and she timed it. Five minutes. As it began to subside, retreating slowly from her fingertips as if she'd taken an aspirin that was just beginning to work, another pain jumped onto her back and began its own digging. This one lasted three minutes, and just as Beth felt the first inklings of relief, another pain began. This one lasted seven minutes. "Regular," the doctor had said.

Beth's newest pain tunneled its way to her eyeballs, and she watched the pink tulips on the shower curtain come suddenly alive. The flower petals split themselves into fingers, each tulip extending its fingers to the others. In a giant circle, with joined hands, the flowers spun fast—a solid, whirling ring. The ring's speed deepened its color to red, then to purple, then propelled the ring from the plastic curtain and into the air of the room. Beth stood, tried to grab hold of the ring, and couldn't. But standing made her water break; it dumped from her fast like an overturned two-liter bottle of soda. She watched it puddle onto the floor, surprised by how much there was, that it was warm and had no color, that it didn't fizz. When she looked back to the shower curtain, the tulips were motionless in their usual places.

"Mom!" she hollered absurdly, half expecting her mother to appear in the bathroom doorway. "My water broke."

She struggled to the phone to call her doctor and a taxicab.

Beth's doctor, upon examining her in the labor and delivery room, said, "You're fully dilated, Liz. We can't give you anything for the pain or your baby will be born floppy." Then the contractions inexplicably stopped and her doctor attached a pitocin IV to her arm. "Your uterus went lazy on us," he said. "We're gonna rev it up with some kick-a-poo juice." She watched the fluid travel through the IV tube into her skin.

The pitocin-induced contractions were louder than screams. Then the pushing blinded her; the pain it caused was red and wrenching and Beth thought she saw her own soul flying from her to escape it. Her soul, she discovered, was not human shaped at all, but an ethereal red ring, like the escaped shower curtain tulips. She reached for her soul as she pushed, trying to pull it back to her body. As she reached, the baby sputtered out of her on a rushing wave of blood and slime. "Kerry," she said, remembering the name from somewhere. Kerry didn't look real at first; she looked rubbery and wet, like an ugly doll some child had abandoned in the rain. Then the ring that was Beth's soul seemed to descend; it wrapped itself around Kerry's head and fell into her mouth. Kerry cried.

The doctor laid Kerry across Beth's stomach for the briefest minute, and Beth was too busy wondering if she herself had died to pay attention to how Kerry felt. A nurse came into the room and was immediately handed the baby. Beth only understood that she was still alive when she heard her doctor say, "I hate to tell you, Liz, but you're still not done. It's time to birth that old placenta."

The afterbirth took a long time to come, and when it finally emerged, enormous and purplish red, Beth couldn't stop looking at it. To her, it looked just *exactly* like a rump roast, and she poked it because she couldn't help herself. It was less dense than a roast; its consistency was more like liver, and it smelled like a horse barn. Beth wished her doctor would explain it to her: which parts of it had been attached to which parts of Kerry and how she could tell. But he only took the placenta away and told her to lie down for her stitches. She lay still and flat, heard Kerry crying and the nurse's voice saying something. She closed her eyes and tried to count the stitches. Her entire pelvic area was numb, so it was hard to differentiate one stitch from another. She thought she counted thirty.

Kerry was asleep by the time Beth's stitches were finished, and she was told to hold her for a minute before the nurses took Kerry away, cleaned her—Beth thought it was her second cleaning but wasn't sure—wrapped her in a blanket, and put her across the room in a clear plastic bassinet, under a lamp. Beth noticed a smell of scrambled eggs in the astringent hospital-room air. She was hungry, but weighed her hunger against her exhaustion before deciding to sleep. Over and over again, she closed her eyes and felt herself travel to the brink of sleeping, but was always recalled by the cold end of a stethoscope on her arm and the squeeze of a blood pressure pump. "It's not falling fast enough," different voices said. Finally, her doctor's face loomed over hers. "You gotta relax, Liz," he said, stroking her hair, his breath stale and sour, like the smell inside a cigar smoker's car. "If your blood pressure doesn't drop, we're gonna have to admit you." She nodded. She couldn't afford to be admitted.

It took ten hours for her blood pressure to return to almost-normal, and when it did, the doctor sent her home. When she got back to her apartment building, Beth carried the baby and the goody bag of diapers and formula she'd gotten from the hospital up the four flights of stairs. With each step, Beth felt her stitches wrench and a heavy gush of hot blood. The stairwell looked foreign to her, and she tried to force herself to recognize it. She tried to remember her apartment number and couldn't. She couldn't remember what her furniture looked like either. The only picture her mind offered was of a mother's dark-sleeved arms: a warm, dry, dark place where she could lie down and heal.

Kerry woke as soon as Beth opened the apartment door. Her little hands shook and her face turned redder than a fire extinguisher. Beth looked around, trying to refamiliarize herself. It wasn't that she didn't remember, she decided. Now that she was looking at her home, nothing about it surprised her. She knew this place, but it seemed that the part of her that knew it was difficult to access, as if it were locked away in some vault of her mind marked "Before." She sat in the rocking chair, holding the stiff and screaming Kerry on the palms of her hands like a serving dish.

"There is such a thing as before and after," she said, repeating something Rachel used to tell her. She half expected Kerry to stop crying the minute she heard her voice, but she didn't. She pulled Kerry close, rocked her back and forth, her stitches pulling as she moved. Kerry's crying didn't change.

"Beth!" her mother might say. "You *are* going to feed the baby, right?"

"Oh," Beth said. "Sorry."

"You're in some daze," her mother's voice sounded in her head.

Beth sat on the couch, lifted her shirt. In the hospital, the nurses had explained breastfeeding to her, but as she tried to do it on her own, she couldn't make sense of her body. First, her arm got in the way of Kerry's head; then, Kerry couldn't seem to take hold of her nipple. She tried to hold her breast and the baby's head steady with one hand while guiding the two together with her other, but wasn't coordinated enough. Kerry's crying escalated and Beth couldn't understand why her instincts didn't kick in and teach her how to do this. It felt like hours of fumbling passed while Kerry screamed. Finally, Kerry locked her mouth onto Beth's nipple. Her grasp was surprisingly strong—it hurt like rug burn. Kerry sucked a couple of times, then stopped and squawked again, her body stiff and hands shaking. Beth put her nipple back in the baby's mouth and felt the burn, tug, and release. More crying.

"What's the matter?" she said aloud, and tried again. This time, Kerry only sucked once before she screamed. Beth squeezed her breast, just to make sure there was milk in it. Nothing came out. "I have no milk!" she said. She squeezed both nipples, hoping for some sort of discharge. There was none. "I have no milk!" she repeated. Kerry screamed in her lap.

She lay the baby down on the floor, stomped into the kitchen, and returned with a baby bottle filled with pre-mixed Similac from the hospital bag. Kerry took the bottle in her mouth, sucking and sighing, eyes closed. Beth watched Kerry's closed-eyed bliss and started crying, sobbing so loudly the noise amazed her. It was not the sound she usually made when she cried; her mother was the one who'd always sobbed aloud. Whenever Beth cried, it was brief and quiet.

"Go pull yourself together, Beth," she whispered to herself in her mother's voice. "We can't have you sitting here going nuts."

In the bathroom, she noticed the crusty spot her water bag had left on the floor. Still crying, she wet a towel in the sink, got on her hands and knees, and mopped the floor clean. Her stitches hurt more in this position and the amount of blood she felt pouring from her made her imagine that her body was no longer a definitive solid. She hypothesized that, instead, she occupied the midpoint between a woman and a puddle of blood and tears. But no milk. Still crying, Beth stood at the sink, splashed cold water on her face, looked in the mirror. Her stomach was still pregnant-pouchy, her hips were wider than a stop sign, but neither of her breasts looked any bigger than they'd ever looked.

Still crying, she took off the bulky diaper-sized maxi pad she'd worn home from the hospital, wrapped it in several layers of toilet paper so she wouldn't smell the blood, and stuck a new pad onto her underwear. She desperately wanted to wash herself but was terrified of the pain, so she dampened a washcloth and patted herself with it a little. The water stung like rubbing alcohol and large maroon blood chunks came off onto the cloth. Bits of afterbirth, Beth hypothesized, and she reluctantly washed the cloth in the bathroom sink. The running water made her feel as though she needed to use the toilet, but she was afraid that would hurt too much, too. She could hear Kerry crying in the living room, remembered that she had nothing to give her, and heard her own crying escalate. She lowered herself onto the toilet.

The temperature of her urine was unbearably hot and hurt enough to make her dizzy. She gripped the side of the bathroom sink, looked at the shower curtain, tried to steady herself. She saw the tulips on the curtain and, for a moment, saw them join hands again to make their ring. She watched their dance, reached for the ring and couldn't catch it. But as she reached, there was a sudden pressure in her breasts as if the tissue had spontaneously calcified into bone. She took her left breast in one hand; at her slightest touch, the milk spurted from her nipple through three ducts. Smiling, she went back into the living room, lifted the crying baby from the floor and attached her to her breast. Kerry closed her eyes and sucked, and with each pull of Kerry's vise-grip mouth, Beth felt her uterus contracting, shrinking, the blood and afterbirth draining from it. Kerry fell asleep in her arms and Beth closed her own eyes and rocked her.

"I've got the hang of it now," Beth said. She imagined her mother answering, "That's what you think."

Kerry still woke every forty-five minutes and Beth still bled when it came time for her six-week post-partum check-up. The doctor didn't seem worried about the blood and told her that women who experienced a lot of tearing bled longer than those who didn't. He said that she could expect to bleed for another couple of weeks, maximum, and gave her a prescription for iron pills, to prevent anemia, he said. Her weight had dropped considerably too; she was only ten pounds heavier than she'd been pre-pregnancy. The doctor smiled about that, called her a "lucky gal," and said, "You'll be back in your Calvin Kleins in no time."

After her appointment, Beth gave the doctor's receptionist the fifty dollars she'd budgeted for the visit.

"It's sixty-five," the receptionist told her.

"Oh," Beth said. "Sorry." In her wallet, she only had twenty dollars left over from her food and diaper money; she'd been planning to use it on diapers—they were almost out—but not seeing any alternative, handed it over. The five dollars she received in change wasn't enough to buy a pack of diapers and there was no place else to go, so she pushed the stroller toward home. It still hurt when she walked and Beth hoped Kerry would stay asleep long enough for her to be able to sneak a nap. The baby woke up the second they got back to the apartment, though, and Beth had to feed her. Then she burped her and changed her diaper. There was only one clean diaper left and Beth didn't how she'd manage to get more. She wouldn't get paid for three days.

She imagined calling Rachel, asking her to come. When she and Rachel were together, Beth had lived in a nicer neighborhood, worked at a better job. Rachel might sit beside her on the couch in this broken-down apartment in one of Chicago's more ragged neighborhoods, her legs crossed in that well-bred way she had. "You were doing so well, Liz," she might say. "You made it out. What happened?"

"What was supposed to happen," Beth answered aloud.

She cooked some rice, balancing Kerry on her hip while she washed the cooking pots. She didn't change Kerry's diaper until the wet soaked through her clothes. Her teeth hurt.

It was midnight before Kerry got to sleep, and Beth sat on the couch, waiting for her to wake again. *I should track down my mother's number somehow; that's what I should do*, she thought, *and demand payback for all the money I gave her.* She imagined her mother opening the front door, smiling at her like a teenager, a plastic bag of diapers looped over one wrist.

"This is your fault," Beth said aloud, as if to her mother's ghost. "You did this to me." Beth tried to imagine the sort of mother she'd have wanted, but no image came to mind. All her imagination offered were those great, dark-sleeved arms, and all the sleep she'd find there.

The baby cried.

"I hear her," Beth said to no one. "I'm up."

Two weeks passed and, despite her doctor's prediction, Beth still bled. During her days and evenings at home, Beth nursed Kerry every half hour, cleaned house, and conducted telephone surveys, phone pressed between her chin and shoulder, one hand writing down whatever data she was given, the other in Kerry's mouth to keep her quiet. At the end of each day, the cartilage of her outer ear felt hot and liquidy, as if any moment it would lose its integrity and drip from her head. She hated the hollow sound of strangers' ringing phones, and the pert answering machine messages that served as windows into brighter lives than hers. She hated when kids answered and didn't know where their mothers were, or when people hung up on her, or yelled at her, or called her names as though she weren't a person on the telephone too.

At night, Kerry woke for feedings every hour. Beth lost another five pounds and the room spun every time she stood. She didn't have enough money to get the iron prescription filled.

One night, Beth woke from a heavy sleep to loud knocking on her apartment door. "It's been forty minutes!" a neighbor bellowed. "Your baby's been crying for forty minutes!"

"I'm sorry," Beth called out, noticing that her heart was beating very fast.

"You've gotta do something about it," the neighbor yelled back. "I work fourteen hour days. I gotta get some sleep."

"I'm a sound sleeper," she answered. "I'm sorry."

In her head, her mother scolded, "You're always sorry."

For the rest of the night, Beth napped on the couch between feedings and found it was easier to wake up when Kerry cried if she was already sitting up with the baby on her lap.

The next morning, when Kerry had sucked for half an hour, Beth noticed that her breasts were empty and she had to stop nursing for several minutes until her milk supply replenished itself. Kerry pointed at her with a rigid finger and hollered. The pointing seemed like something her mother would do, though she'd never seen her mother point. She noticed that, even when her breasts had refilled and Kerry had been reattached to them, her daughter's pointing finger stayed upright. It only curled down to rejoin the ball of her fist when she fell asleep.

Beth spent that night sleep-sitting on the couch too. During Kerry's 1:30 AM feeding, Beth felt her breasts completely drained long before they ought to have been. When her milk came back, Kerry only sucked a few minutes before it depleted again. Beth could feel that her breasts were empty, but Kerry kept sucking without complaint so she let her nurse through the dry spell and, eventually, felt her milk return. But as her new milk came in, an electric pain exploded in her mouth, as if all her teeth were shattering at the roots. Instinctively, she put her finger on the sorest place—the gumline immediately above her far-thest upper right molar. She pressed down to assuage the pain and the tooth popped out whole like an ice cube from a tray. There wasn't very much blood and she felt what little there was slide down her throat. Beth held the lost tooth in her hand and gently tugged at all her other teeth. Several of them felt loose.

There was no milk in the house, so after Kerry had gone back to sleep, Beth ferreted through the hospital goody bag for a can of Similac and drank it. The formula had a grainy texture and an after-taste like a multi-vitamin. She took one more can out of the hos-pital goody bag and drank that too. Then she dropped her lost tooth through one of the can's pull-tab holes and buried both empty cans at the very bottom of the trash can under the dinner scraps and dirty diapers.

When Kerry woke for her 5:00 AM feeding, Beth noticed that nursing didn't hurt her teeth so much and that her milk lasted longer. She fell back to sleep when Kerry did and, when she woke again, was amazed that Kerry had managed to sleep for two consecutive hours so far. It was the formula, Beth decided, wondering how she'd manage to buy more. She'd already spent this week's grocery money.

By Kerry's midday feeding, Beth's teeth hurt again. She thought of the men with missing teeth her mother used to date; Beth had always blamed their tooth loss on drugs. But now here she was with her teeth falling out, no dental insurance, no money and not a drop of milk in the house. She held the baby and cried. Kerry pointed at her. She seemed to be saying to shut up.

Beth said, "My teeth are falling out of my head, Kerry. I'll be a jack o' lantern by five o'clock if I don't get some Similac." Then she packed Kerry into her stroller and, dizzy and bleeding, carried the stroller down the apartment steps, rolled it down the street and stole a six-pack of Similac from the corner store before she'd decided on that course of action. The man at the cash register was on the phone and didn't look up. Beth braced herself for the blare of some hidden alarm system, but when she was two steps onto the sidewalk and no alarm sounded, she ran as fast as she could, bleeding with every step and jostling Kerry to tears. Out of breath, she sat on the curb in front of her apartment building, opened the first can of Similac, and drank it in two gulps. She left the empty can at her feet, panted until she caught her breath, then opened another can and drank that too. When she stood up, she noticed a patch of blood on the curb and that her pants were wet.

She called her doctor when she got home. When she told him about the blood, he said she should get herself "to an emergent care center and pronto." Then she told him about the tooth she'd lost and asked what might be wrong. He only repeated, "Pronto."

After she hung up, she realized she'd forgotten to ask how much going to the emergency room might cost.

She went to the bathroom and changed her maxi-pad, underwear, and pants. Maybe she'd just gone too long on one pad, she thought. Maybe she always bled this much and was mistaking bad hygiene for something worse. While she was getting dressed, Kerry woke and started crying. Beth tried giving her a bottle of Similac, but she wouldn't take it. So she put the bottle in her own mouth and drank it while Kerry nursed. The pain in her teeth, uterus, and nipples made her feel as if her body was splitting into pieces. Kerry continued nursing and Beth thought she saw her soul leaving her body through the open places. It rose above her head and made a purple, spinning ring. "I thought you were gone," Beth said to the ring that was her soul. "I thought you left me when Kerry was born."

"I would never leave you, Beth," she heard the ring answer. It had her mother's voice.

She watched the ring spinning faster and faster above her head while Kerry nursed. She felt the blood pour from her like paint from an overturned bucket. She opened another can of Similac and drank it. Kerry continued to nurse. She closed her eyes and was surprised that she could still see the ring, that in fact it looked even brighter now and was changing shape. The ring grew flatter and more opaque. *It looks like the afterbirth*, Beth thought, and she imagined crawling inside it. She reached for it but couldn't catch it. By touch, she switched Kerry to her other breast, groped for another can of Similac, opened it. Maybe this was all just malnutrition? Well, she was fixing that.

The Shell Game

News that her mother needed money and news of her arrival came in the same telegram, postmarked Pittsburgh, Pennsylvania, because her mother had already left Jersey City. Today, Beth would meet her mother at the Chicago Greyhound station. She carried five hundred dollars in her left sock.

The telegram arrived yesterday. After reading it, she collected all the money she could find, including quarters scavenged from the pockets of forgotten jackets. Then she bought new pants: expensive, pleated, lined pants, the sort a lady doctor might wear on her day off. Their price tag was attached with a straight pin. Forty dollars. Close-out. Marked down from a hundred and ten. Now, she wished for a more prosperous-looking overcoat. The fabric of her coat shone at the elbows, and its awkwardly colored replacement buttons were too big for the buttonholes. Beth hadn't seen her mother since the last time her mother needed money, over three years ago, when her mother pretended to be dead, before Beth's daughter was born. According to the telegram, her mother would be in town for forty minutes. It was only enough time for her to take Beth's money and go.

She'd left Kerry, her two-year-old, at home with a babysitter. The babysitter was a woman from work named Donna—a beautiful, older woman who moved about easily, offering warm, clean smiles. Sometimes, at work, Beth invented reasons to visit Donna in her office and, during one of those visits, not long ago, Beth managed to lean her head against Donna's soft, clean shoulder for many seconds before Donna ruffled her hair and pulled away, smiling. "Silly girl," she'd said, and Beth felt ashamed of the way she must have looked at Donna; she'd probably given Donna the same look she'd once given to Gina, her first lover, and, later, to Rachel, her second. Donna's hands, meticulously manicured, smelled slightly of lemon.

Donna, women, the office, Beth's second-wave poverty, and even Kerry were all parts of the life Beth's mother had never asked to see. So she would keep it all a secret: her daughter, her job, her longings, her apartment and its water-stained walls and broken stove, her ragged North Chicago neighborhood and its boarded-up used-to-be grocery stores. She wouldn't tell her mother that the neighborhood wasn't even cheap, that she could barely afford to pay for food and rent even though she worked full-time down the hall from Donna's office, answering phones.

Before her mother pretended to be dead, before Kerry, Beth had some money, a job as an office manager, and a beautiful, smart lady lover named Rachel. Then she abandoned everything and worked at home, conducting telephone surveys until Kerry turned two and was old enough, finally, to start a preschool Beth could nearly afford. Now, Beth was back to office work and starting over. Kerry's preschool cost two hundred dollars a week, even though it only offered days of soggy toast and stained linoleum. But she wouldn't tell her mother that. Instead, she'd present herself in new, black pants and try to hide the ugly buttons of her overcoat as she extended a wad of cash. She'd never tell her mother that the money was what she would have used toward this month's rent.

She awaited the elevated train, two stops north of the end of the line. The platform smelled of tar and winter, and Beth stood in a wind shelter, shivering beneath buzzing heat lamps. Inside the train hung advertisements for bill consolidation companies, discount divorces, women's clinics. One advertisement pictured a young woman hugging her knees. PREGNANT? read the caption. Beside that question, in black magic marker, someone had written, TRUST JESUS.

Later, at the Greyhound station, Beth's mother would describe, in a dramatic and pitiful voice, how she'd sent the telegram from the Western Union window at the Pittsburgh bus depot then walked two blocks to the Marriott Hotel. She would tearfully describe white

Christmas lights flickering everywhere in the frigid Pennsylvania air. She would wipe her eyes and say that she had been on a bus for two days already and had not slept. If only she could have afforded a plane! The bus was so dirty, she'd say. And because she felt dirty—so dirty she'd repeat—from riding the bus, she washed her hair in the bathroom sink of the Marriott's lobby. Imagine that, she'd cry; what kind of life do I have that, at my age, I have to ride buses instead of planes and wash my hair in public sinks?

Sometimes Beth imagined the boxed-in futility of her mother's life until she cried.

The train headed south, past the northside annex of Chinatown, the Uptown projects, a city community college with a sign that, for years, had been missing three letters from its name, past streets filled with supermercados and broken glass and old elementary schools with BOYS' ENTRANCE and GIRLS' ENTRANCE etched into crumbling cement walls. A vast cemetery separated Uptown from Wrigley Field and the posh neighborhoods to its immediate south. Long ago, Beth had lived in one of these neighborhoods. This was the kind of neighborhood, she imagined, Donna lived in now. She noticed the quiet ballfield, closed for the winter, the linen-table restaurants, the vintage clothing boutiques. Christmas wreaths hung from gray, steel lampposts in the flat, gray air.

The train stopped at a sparsely populated platform. A young couple boarded. The boy looked anachronistically clean-cut; his pink scalp shone through his short hair, and his face looked as if he'd scoured it. He could have been the subject of an old photograph: Naval cadet on weekend leave. His girl looked like a picture too; she kept her yellow hair pushed back from her face with a red headband that matched her overcoat and gloves. She held the boy's elbow when they sat down in the seat in front of Beth. A woman wearing layers of ragged cardigans instead of a coat took the seat beside her. She smelled of cold air and stale cigarettes. Another ragged passenger, a man, sat across the aisle. He set a small wooden board across his knees, took three bottle caps and a marble from his jacket pocket, hid the marble beneath one of the bottle caps, and arranged the caps on the board.

"What'cha doin'?" the woman beside Beth asked the man.

This old game. Beth looked out the window. She could see where the city streets met Lake Michigan's desolate silver water.

Forty minutes wasn't even long enough to leave the bus station to talk over lunch at a diner down the street. Instead, they'd spend it standing on line inside the terminal, waiting for the bus to be refueled, waiting for a new bucket of rank blue water to replace the even more rank bucket that had served as the bus's toilet since New Hampshire. They'd stand among passengers whose children, desperate to finally control their own movement, circled their heels. Beth would give her mother the money but it wouldn't be enough to fix anything. Perhaps, she thought, it would be enough if she were someone else, someone clean and radiantly at ease, like Donna. But she was not like Donna, so perhaps, instead, the help she had to offer would somehow turn wretched, and two days from now, her mother's head would begin to itch. Maybe by the time her mother arrived in California or wherever she was going this time, she'd scratch her head and find lice beneath her fingernails.

"A woman on the northbound train just won a hundred bucks!" the man with the board across his knees announced as he began moving the bottle caps around. "Watch the ball, watch the ball. Which one is it under? Watch the ball."

The ragged passenger beside Beth leaned toward him. "It's under that one." She pointed to a bottle cap.

The man lifted it to reveal the marble. "If you'd been playing for cash you'd have cleaned me out!"

"How much to play?" the boy in front of Beth asked.

"Don't," his yellow-haired girlfriend warned in a surprisingly deep voice. "I've known this game all my life."

"Let him play if he wants to," the man with the board said.

"I'll play if he don't," the woman beside Beth offered, and before she could even finish the sentence, the man with the board exhorted,

"Good girl! You play!"

They're working together, Beth decided. This woman would win a few rounds to make the boy think the game was fair, then they'd rob the boy blind.

"Low bid's twenty bucks," the man continued. "You show me your twenty, you get it right, I match your twenty. You get it wrong, I keep it."

"Okay."

"Okay!" He moved the bottle caps. "Where's the ball? Where's the ball? Watch the ball."

"It's there." The woman pointed to one of the caps.

"Put your twenty up," the man replied.

She rummaged through her purse and held up a wrinkled bill. "Here's my twenty."

The man took it from her. "Show me the ball and you get it back plus another one."

"I already showed you. It's there." She pointed again to the cap she chose. The boy turned in his seat to watch. It had all been pre-arranged, Beth knew. The marble would be under the cap, and the boy would decide to play.

The man lifted the cap. "Nothing," he said.

"But it was there." The woman's voice was raspy, panicked.

"It was here." He lifted a different cap. "You wanna chance to win it back? If you got another twenty you can play again."

She searched quickly through her purse. "I've just got a five."

"I'll let you play with a five."

"What can I do?"

This time, the man moved the bottle caps faster. So they weren't cohorts after all. Beth wished the boy had played instead.

The ragged woman lifted her five dollar bill and made her guess. There was nothing beneath the bottle cap she chose.

"That's all the money I have," she pleaded. "You have to let me play again. I have to win it back."

"You can't play if you can't pay," the man said.

"I got kids," she said. "It was all I had."

"I didn't make you play," the man rejoined, not meeting her eyes.

"You gotta help me," she persisted, leaning across the aisle toward the man, her hands practically resting on the gameboard.

The man put the bottle caps and marble back in his pocket and moved his board out of her reach. He took stereo headphones from another pocket and put them on.

"Oh please, God, somebody help me." The woman put her face in her hands. Then she glanced at Beth. "Please, Miss?"

Beth considered taking a bill from her sock, playing until she won back everything the woman beside her spent, playing until she had a thousand dollars, enough for her mother and the rent. But she wouldn't win because no one ever won this game. She imagined what Donna would say if Beth came home and admitted to having lost all her money on the shell game. She imagined how her mother might turn her back and ask her to leave if she didn't have the cash. "I wish I could," she said.

"Yes?" The woman's voice raised hopefully.

"I wish I could," Beth repeated.

"You can? Please?"

Beth shook her head and looked away. Out the train window, she saw the clean, brick buildings of a private university. The Days Inn stood alongside the university, serving businessmen and parents of coeds. She used to see a man, Kerry's father, in that hotel, long ago, before Kerry was born. This was something else her mother would never know. The man was much older, married, and paid Beth well. His wife was a lady doctor.

"You're so pale," Kerry's father had said the first time she went to his room. "Come in and lie down. You'll feel better."

Once they had gone to bed four times, Beth felt the irrepressible need to say, "You should be faithful to your lady doctor instead. It would save you money."

"You just don't want me," he answered. "Just say that."

"Want?" she repeated. It wasn't about what she wanted. There seemed to be a correct course of events that existed regardless of her wants. It seemed correct, for example, that someone who paid her for sex would not do so at the expense of someone worthier than she.

The elevated track sloped downward into a dark concrete subway tunnel. The train grew louder underground; suddenly audible were the electric screeches of wheels against tracks, the hollow moan of air being cut by the train. But it was still possible to hear the woman beside Beth asking, "Can you help me, Miss? You want to help me, don't you please?"

The young boy seated in front of Beth let go of his girl's arm. He lurched down the aisle, removed the other man's headphones and hollered, "This is insane! Give her the money back."

"I didn't make her play," the man repeated smoothly. "You want her to get her money back, you win it back."

"If that's how, that's how," the boy said. "What did she lose? Twenty-five?"

"Don't be an idiot," his girlfriend said. "He keeps the ball in his pocket. It's not under any of them."

"I'm square," the man protested, setting up his gameboard and bottle caps again. "I don't do anybody that way. I'm square."

"Put it under a cap," the boy said. "I want to see it's there."

The man placed the marble beneath one of the caps. "Satisfied?"

The boy nodded and the man started spinning the bottle caps. The boy lost twenty dollars. "Go again," he said. "I'll bet ten."

"Stop," his girlfriend told him. "Please."

In only a few stops, Beth would get off this subway and switch to another. She would walk to the other platform through a fetid underground tunnel, past a man standing against the damp concrete wall, singing doo-wop, head thrown back, a hat between his feet for coins. Once she was on the second train, the bus station was only two stops away. Maybe her mother would be traveling with a lover, another one of those toothless boys who slapped her mother's ass and called her baby. Or maybe she had just left one in New Jersey, or was en route toward a new one now.

The boy continued playing, betting on bottle cap after bottle cap, losing one bill after the next. "This game is rigged!" he complained.

"I told you," his girlfriend said. "You're such a moron. I told you it isn't even under there."

"It is. It is. I'm square," the man with the gameboard replied. "You just gotta keep your eye on it."

"Go to hell," the girl said, standing, pulling the boy to his feet. The train stopped beneath the Magnificent Mile. In the subway tunnel, people in smart coats holding crisp white shopping bags waited for the train doors to open. Before leaving the train, the boy who'd lost his money looked at the woman next to Beth. His face was as red as his girlfriend's coat. He handed her a ten-dollar bill. "It's all I have left," he said. "Sorry I couldn't win it back for you."

"God bless you," she replied. "God bless you for trying."

The shoppers filled the train, clogged the aisles. They rested their bags between their feet, held the subway poles with leather gloves. Beth thought of the woman next to her; she'd be unable to make a holiday for her kids. But Beth couldn't afford to make one for Kerry, either. It was good Kerry was still too little to notice. Maybe there would be someone to help someday. Maybe when she got back home today, Donna would let Beth rest her head against her shoulder and then her neck and then her breasts. Or maybe, when Beth's mother outgrew desire, when there were no more men to meet, she'd remember the money Beth gave and gave her, and she'd send a different kind of telegram, one that announced she'd given up the worst of her habits, and, transformed, was coming to help at last and to stay.

"How old are your kids?" Beth asked the woman, but she was standing, pressing her way through the aisle, leaving the train one stop before Beth's. The man with the gameboard was leaving, too. Through the train window, Beth saw them standing close together. The man smiled at the woman, patted her cheek, and they walked hand in hand toward the steps that led up to the street.

The train neared Beth's stop. They *were* working together, then, cashing in on other people's sympathy. It was a new twist to Beth;

she'd never seen the scam engineered in that way. It was a good way to earn some cash, really, she thought. They shouldn't have gotten off the train. They should have kept playing.

The Cat

They'd been here since dark because her mother said kittens were nocturnal and would most easily be found at night, but they'd seen no kittens at all in her father's enormous backyard. Hours ago, Kerry and her mother had sneaked over the chain-link fence and tiptoed across the vast expanse of long grass like burglars because the gates were locked, and they'd been sitting stock still on the ground near the back edge of the yard ever since, their flashlights pointed toward the overgrown, sprawling hedge under which, two weekends ago, Kerry had seen the kittens for the first and only time. They'd set out plates of milk and tuna in hopes of tempting the kittens into the open. Perhaps, Kerry thought, even more hours would pass before the kittens got hungry enough to come. Perhaps if it got late enough, her mother would, for once, call out sick from work tomorrow and, for once, let Kerry stay home from school. She'd been at her father's house all weekend, living among the prickly mysteries and quiet odors of this other family to whom she belonged, and a day at home with her mother and a kitten would make her feel a little more normal.

At her father's, the plates matched, the forks gleamed, and breakfast juice was served in smaller glasses than the ones used at other times of day. At her father's, everyone ate meals together, something Kerry and her mother never did at home. At home, her mother, still in her work clothes and stockings, cooked something fast and brought a plate for Kerry into Kerry's bedroom. Kerry ate while doing homework, her television on, while her mother changed into sweatpants and took a nap on the living room couch. At her father's, Kerry, her father, and Margaret, her father's wife, ate lunch and dinner in the dining room and breakfast in what Margaret called "the nook," a kind of booth in the kitchen.

Her father and his wife were old. They had a daughter who was older than Kerry's mother, a daughter named Alethia whom Kerry had never met, though Kerry, on the weekends she visited, slept across the hall from Alethia's old bedroom, which looked as though it were waiting for the arrival of a princess. In Alethia's bedroom, Kerry had once lifted a porcelain-faced doll from a shelf mounted to the wall; Margaret saw her holding the doll, took it gently away and said, "That's your sister's, sweetie. We'll get you one of your own for Christmas." At her father's, there were always presents or promises of presents, and there was always the mention of Alethia, who seemed to haunt the quiet rooms with her absence. During the long hours Kerry spent visiting, she wanted only to go home to the small apartment she and her mother shared. But when, on Sunday afternoons, her mother arrived to retrieve her, their old car popping and huffing up the quiet street, and her father said, "I hear Liz!" in a voice that sounded as though it were making fun of everything, Kerry wanted to stay.

Her mother would ring her father's front doorbell and Kerry would stand between Margaret and her father in the foyer, looking through the storm door's glass at her mother on the porch. And Kerry would feel hatred for her mother rise as a big, red bubble in her throat. But looking at her mother's tired eyes always made the bubble dissolve. It wasn't *her* hatred, she'd invariably decide. It was her father's. It had to be. And she'd dash outside, arms extended hopefully.

"Ready?" her mother would always say without smiling, and she'd take Kerry's overnight bag from one of those outstretched arms and Kerry would follow her to the car and back into a life of dilapidated, familiar things.

Even food was fancy at her father's. Kerry ate things she'd never heard of and was expected to finish everything on her plate. Whenever she complained about this to her mother, her mother only said, "Remember to be polite." Whenever she complained about this to her father, her father said, "I don't know what Liz lets you get away with, pumpkin, but we clean our plates in this house," while Margaret looked at her as though getting ready to cry and said, "You're tall.

You need to eat." In the framed photographs on every wall of her father's house, Alethia looked skinny, all big eyes and bony knees. "Did Alethia have to eat everything?" Kerry had once asked Margaret, and Margaret had made an abrupt, sucking sound and answered, "Your sister had a little problem with food." But the exact nature of that problem remained unspoken, just as the reason Alethia never came home remained unspoken. Unspoken, too, was how her father and mother could possibly have had an acquaintance that ended in Kerry's birth, why her father hadn't been part of Kerry's life until Kerry was six years old, or why her father seemed to make Kerry hate her mother so very much.

That hatred had gotten her mother to agree to look for the kittens. At first, her mother had said no. "We can't," she'd said. Their car had struggled its way onto the freeway that separated the suburbs from the city. "I'm too tired and we'll never find them." So Kerry, through that awful red bubble, had repeated something she'd once overheard her father and Margaret say, though she hadn't been certain they'd said it about her mother. "What's trailer trash, Mother?"

Her mother sighed, and, not looking at her, said, "All right. But kittens are nocturnal. After dark, when they're awake, we'll go back and look for them."

The kittens' mother had died this morning, presumably while Kerry and Margaret and her father ate breakfast in the nook and Margaret, as was her custom at meals, asked Kerry question after question. How was school, how were her friends, how were her grades, had she finished her homework? These questions were always difficult for Kerry. She didn't like her private Catholic girls' school where everyone wore uniforms, talked of God as though he were real, and walked through hallways that smelled like the inside of someone's mouth, but she knew Margaret and her father paid for her to go there and that her mother would want her to be polite. So she talked about the final project she was working on for math class now that fourth grade was coming to an end, the books she was reading, the few friends she had. She didn't tell Margaret how the other girls made fun of her—for being tall, for having a single mother, for living in an apartment, for liking to read. Margaret's questions were difficult, but not nearly as difficult as the ones her father asked immediately afterward, the questions about her mother ("dear old Liz" her father called her), which were impossible to answer correctly. Neither saying that her mother was fine nor complaining about her seemed to make her father happy.

This morning when her father asked, "And how is dear, old Liz?" Kerry answered, "She's tired." It was the best she could do.

"Spends a lot of time in bed from what I hear," Margaret chimed in, looking at Kerry's father.

"On the couch, actually," Kerry said. But neither Margaret nor her father seemed to be listening.

"Statute of limitations," her father said to Margaret. Then to Kerry, he said, "Do you want more bacon, pumpkin? There's more. Isn't there, Margaret?"

"Of course," Margaret said. Then, smiling kindly at Kerry, she said, "I can cook some up for you if you're still hungry."

Kerry didn't know whether she wanted more bacon or not. She thought of her mother's tired eyes and desperate requests that Kerry be polite. "I'm fine," she assured Margaret. "Honest."

But Margaret was already moving toward the stove.

"She says she doesn't want more," Kerry's father said.

"Nonsense. She's tall. She needs to eat."

"I'm fine," Kerry said again. She brought her dirty dishes to the sink and rinsed them.

"Leave them," Margaret said. "I'll throw them in the dishwasher."

There wasn't a dishwasher at her mother's; at her mother's, they washed dishes by hand. "It's okay. It's no trouble." When she spent weekends with Margaret and her father, Kerry sometimes wanted to bring home everything they owned to make her mother's life easier. Then, when she got home, she sometimes wanted to scream at her mother, "Why can't you afford a dishwasher like at Daddy's?"

"Oh no!" Margaret shouted, and Kerry jumped. She looked at the plate in her hands. Had she broken it without noticing? But

Margaret was standing at the front window. "Mark!" she said.

Her father came to the window too, and Kerry followed.

"No," Kerry's father said. "Stay there." But Kerry didn't hear him in time and, through the window, saw the dead cat lying in the street. Kerry had discovered the cat in her father's backyard around Christmastime. Every weekend she'd visited, she'd sat outside for hours, coaxing the cat closer and closer with saucers of milk and plates of tuna while Margaret left the house for the hospital where she worked as a doctor, and her father went to play racquetball. Or sometimes, while Kerry sat outside taming the cat, they stayed inside the house, Margaret reading in the study, her father watching television in the den or exercising on the sleek black machines in the basement. Just two months ago, the cat had finally allowed Kerry to pet her. Her hard belly bulged.

"I think she's pregnant," Kerry told her father.

He shook his head. "It's probably just worms."

"Can we bring her inside?" Kerry asked Margaret. "You could help her have her kittens, right?"

"No, sweetie," Margaret answered. "We don't know anything about her. And your dad and I just aren't home enough when you're not here."

When her mother came to retrieve her that Sunday afternoon, when she stood at the front door and asked Margaret, "Was she good?" as she always did, Kerry didn't go outside right away. Instead, as she stood between Margaret and her father, she asked through the storm door whether she could bring the pregnant cat home. Her mother looked at her and said, "What about our security deposit, Kerry? Birth is messy. Besides, if anyone found out, we could get evicted."

"You shouldn't say stuff like that to her," Kerry's father snapped. He ruffled Kerry's hair with a large, warm hand. "You're not going to get evicted, pumpkin."

"I know what we should do," Margaret offered. "We should take her to a vet. Depending on how far along she is, it might not be too late to spay her."

"What? Abort the kittens?" Kerry's mother asked.

"Well, it's better than having them born to a stray. We don't know anything about her. She's half feral. She could have all kinds of problems."

"No!" Kerry said. "There's nothing wrong with her. I can tell."

"Margaret's right." Kerry's mother looked down and bit her lower lip.

"I'll take a kitten," Kerry said. "I'll take two."

"We'll buy you a kitten, pumpkin," her father said.

"But I want one of those kittens."

"Sweetie," Margaret said. "If we let her have her kittens, most of them probably won't survive. And the ones that do could have whatever diseases she's got, and they'll wind up just as feral as she is."

"Margaret's right," Kerry's mother said again.

"We don't even know that she's pregnant," her father said, as if scolding everyone. "It's too early in the year for kittens. I'm telling you, she probably just has worms."

But Margaret told Kerry to try to catch the cat anyhow and promised she'd bring her to the vet that very day. Kerry found an old, ratty Winnie the Pooh towel in the very back of the upstairs linen closet to wrap around the cat, but Margaret said, "Wait, sweetie. Use a different towel." And she brought Kerry a much newer towel instead, one with Margaret and her father's initials sewn into the fabric.

Kerry and her mother walked around her father's yard, among grass, knee-high weeds, and several shrubs taller than either of them. Behind the back fence, an acre of trees grew, one of the suburb's remaining tiny forests. On her father's side of the fence stood an enormous hedge, its chaotic branches wrapping themselves around every non-living thing in their reach. That morning, Kerry had put bowls of food beneath the hedge's lowest branches for the cat to eat happily while Kerry pet her, but now the cat was nowhere. "We have to get going," her mother finally said, and Margaret promised she'd continue searching for the cat herself. Evidently, she'd never found the cat or had never really looked because when Kerry saw the cat again, her belly was flat. She ate an enormous bowl of food as though starving, and Kerry could feel the cat's nipples when she pet her belly.

"It wasn't worms," she told her father.

But the cat stayed in the yard for hours and her father said the kittens had probably all died.

"I don't know," Margaret said. "Cats can leave their babies alone for pretty long periods of time."

"Not that long," her father countered. "She's been out back all day."

Then, two weeks ago, four little kittens—two orange tabbies, a gray tabby and a calico—tottered maladroitly from under the big hedge at the back of the yard when Kerry brought a bowl of food out for their mother. Kerry moved toward the kittens, but their mother hissed dangerously and the kittens fled to the apparent safety of the branches. The mother cat, nicer when her kittens weren't around, stayed near Kerry, eating and purring while Kerry pet her. She rubbed her mouth against Kerry's hand in a desperate show of affection. Now the cat was dead.

Kerry ran outside, into the street where the cat lay. She'd evidently been hit by a car; her body looked strange—rigid and small—and one of her eyes stuck halfway out of her eye socket. *Eyeball*, Kerry thought. It was the first time she'd ever realized the appropriateness of the word. *Eyeball*. Even hours later, it was what she remembered best about the cat's sad carcass.

"We need to get the kittens," she told Margaret and her father. "They're in the hedge. That's where she hid them."

"She may have moved them, sweetie," Margaret warned. "Sometimes animals move their young."

"They won't survive without her, that's for sure," her father said. "They'll become some other animal's dinner."

Now, Kerry feared her father was right. She and her mother hadn't spoken or moved in hours, and although it was May, the nighttime air was cold. The sky looked different out here in the suburbs, darker and full of stars. In the city, the sky was always pink and starless, even at midnight. Everything was quiet here too, as though nothing lived anywhere for miles around.

"Do you think we'll find them, Mother?"

"I don't know."

Just then, the sound of movement in the grass behind them made Kerry turn, hopefully. "Listen!"

"Shhh," her mother said. "Quietly or we'll scare them."

But Kerry's flashlight illuminated not a kitten but her father striding angrily toward them in his bare feet and pajamas. "What the hell is wrong with you, Liz?" he yelled.

Kerry ran to him, her finger over her lips. Her legs felt stiff from sitting still. "The kittens," she whispered.

But her father didn't keep quiet. "You didn't call, Liz? You just came out here without calling? What'd you do, climb the fence?"

Kerry's mother nodded.

Across the yard, the house came to life with light; the backyard lights turned on, and Kerry knew that the kittens, if they were anywhere around, would be too scared to come out. And now Margaret, in her nightclothes too, walked toward them with something in her hand.

"Here," she said, handing Kerry and her mother strange headbands with flashlights attached to them. They looked like something a coal miner would wear.

"We bought these as a Christmas gift for Alethia a few years back," Margaret said. "In case she likes to go camping now." Then she looked a little sheepishly at Kerry and smiled. "You can use them anyway, sweetie. You'll need your hands free if the kittens come out."

"The kittens are gone," Kerry's father said. "They haven't been seen in weeks and their mother's been dead since this morning."

Kerry slipped the lamp around her head. The effect was amazing. Unlike a flashlight's impotent singular beam, the headlamp seemed to invest her eyes with new powers. The yard looked as bright as it would at four in the afternoon. *This must be how a cat sees at night*, she thought.

"You don't know that they're gone," Margaret said. "Not every wild creature becomes something lost for you to romanticize."

"What's romanticize?" Kerry asked. Beside her, her mother had gone very, very still. Kerry walked toward the hedge; she could see every rock on the ground.

"Nothing," her mother answered. "If she really thinks that, it's because your father told her lies about me."

"About you?" Kerry's father said. "She wasn't alluding to you."

"Oh," Kerry's mother said. "I'm sorry."

"You've got problems, Liz," her father said.

"I'm sorry," her mother repeated. "I know I do."

Kerry felt her hatred—her *father's* hatred, she corrected herself—rise in her throat again. *He doesn't realize that she's good,* she thought. *She's so tired but she came to look for the kittens anyway.* In the glow from her headlamp, she saw a row of reflected eyes moving toward her father's yard from the small forest behind it. She held her breath, but as the creatures moved closer to the fence, Kerry saw that they weren't kittens at all, but raccoons: a large mother and three babies.

"It's too early in the year for baby raccoons," Kerry's father said.

"Apparently not, Mark," Margaret rejoined.

The mother raccoon reached the fence and began to climb, her dexterous paws clinging to the chain-link. When she got about halfway up, she reached down to one of her babies who grasped her fingers as a human might and began to climb the fence too.

"Aren't they afraid of us?" Kerry's mother asked.

"They're beautiful," Margaret said, and Kerry felt Margaret's hand on her shoulder. "Look how she helps them climb. I didn't know they did that."

Kerry shrugged Margaret's hand away. "Those raccoons can't come here," she said. "They'll eat the kittens."

"Those kittens are long gone, pumpkin," her father said. "I'm sorry."

"You don't know that," Kerry said. "You always say that you know things and then you're wrong. You don't know anything."

"Kerry," her mother warned. "Be polite."

Kerry swallowed hard, but the red bubble wouldn't budge. "You don't know anything either," she said.

Two weeks from now, Kerry's father would take her to a posh pet store where Kerry would choose a sleek, gray tabby kitten for her father to buy. Her mother would say, "He couldn't have gotten one from the pound, at least?" and Kerry would answer, "Oh, Mother. Be polite." Her mother would pet the kitten and ask, "What's his name?" And Kerry would say, "Sam," as Sam hopped onto their battered living room couch as if he'd always belonged there. Two weeks from now, Kerry would understand that the kittens in her father's yard were lost for good.

But right now, as a second baby raccoon began its climb up the chain-link, Kerry only knew she needed to keep them from entering the yard. She shone her headlamp at the ground and gathered some big rocks, which she threw, hard, at the mother raccoon.

"Don't," Margaret said.

"She's right, Margaret," said Kerry's mother. "If there *are* still kittens, the raccoons are interfering with the goal." And all the adults—even Kerry's father, even Margaret—threw rocks at the fence until the raccoons retreated back into the trees.

Read Me Through the Bardo, Won't You?

I remember when you asked me to read you through the Bardo. You knew about the Bardo. You could not always make it to the bathroom. You could not keep a job or file your taxes or fill out your own Public Aid paperwork, but you knew about the Bardo. Sometimes I thought that the person who knew things was the real you, and that all that helplessness was just pretense. But just in case your helplessness was real, I'm here to read you through...

Tuesday

This is the kind of news that should be told face-to-face, Beth thought. She sat on her daughter's bedroom floor, on the telephone with the police. They always used the phone in Kerry's room because it had the apartment's only working jack. *There should be some kind of law protecting people from having to hear about death, motherhood, and other catastrophes over the telephone.* Into the receiver, she asked questions like, "Was her boyfriend there at the time?" She wasn't crying.

The police officer said the word "troubled." He asked, "Did your mother ever take anything for depression?"

"She self-medicated," Beth answered.

"With street drugs."

"Yes."

They couldn't afford to run the air conditioner, and Beth was sweating so much that bits of carpet stuck to her legs. Ten days ago, when her mother had put the mouth of a gun into her own mouth and pulled the trigger, it was still cold in Chicago. Beth had worn sweaters through the end of June. But now it was early July and suddenly summer. The day before she learned of her mother's death, when life still felt benign and ordinary, Kerry and Beth had discussed where to buy an electric fan now that the neighborhood's only department and hardware stores had closed to make way for a parking garage. After hanging up the phone and walking lightly, strangely through the hallway that seemed too bright, Beth found Kerry sitting on the living room couch, sweating too, making herself even warmer by clutching the fat tabby cat, Sam, on her lap. Baby clothes that she'd bought from resale shops lay around her feet.

"That was the police," Beth had said, her voice seeming to travel from far away. "About your grandmother." The word sounded foreign, a lie. Beth's mother had never met Kerry, nor asked to meet her.

"What I think he'd like now is some marshmallow ice cream," Kerry said, reaching into the pile of baby clothes for a bib to fasten around Sam's neck. "Is your mother in trouble?"

"He's already too fat. Ice cream's no good for him. Can't you do that with a doll or something? Look how he hates it." Sam fixed his long-suffering eyes on Beth and uttered a pitiful mewl of protest.

"I'm too old for dolls. Anyway, Mother, it's not as if I'm playing dress-up with him. We have a bond, Sammy and me. This is how we communicate."

"I'm going for a walk," Beth said. *Twelve is a strange age*, she decided, *Too much of a crossroads.* The little girl and adolescent parts of Kerry's identity seemed to be trying, somehow, to make a sensible whole. "Leave him alone if he starts getting riled."

"He's my cat, Mother." But she let go of Sam. "So what happened with your mother?"

"I don't know exactly," Beth said. "I think she's dead." But her mother had pretended to be dead before now. Thirteen years ago. It was a fake doctor who'd called then, not the real cops. And the doctor hadn't given Beth a phone number or any kind of proof.

"Oh Mommy." Kerry stood and pulled Beth toward her with long arms. Kerry had always been too tall for her age; now, she was taller than Beth. Kerry hugged hard, the way little children do, but her size made it feel frightening, as if Beth would disappear forever. Kerry smelled overly sweet, like a baby, and her big hands were sticky from ice cream.

"Mommy can't breathe," she said, pulling away. If Kerry were smaller, Beth could have held her and found comfort. "I'm going to go for a walk. No ice cream for Sam, all right?"

"All right." Kerry went down the hall to her room and Beth heard the stereo come on; the grating thump of a drum machine backed up a hip-hop singer's taunt, "What the fuck? Is you stupid?"

You told me about the Bardo in a Jersey City welfare office. I remember the office, how lots of women and an occasional man occupied row after row of stiff metal chairs. I remember children—some clean and wearing crisp, ironed outfits washed in bleach, some with small bits of wet snacks balled in their fists and smeared across their faces and shirts— climbing on the women and one another. Some of the women hollered or threatened spankings or picked their children up to coddle them. Some acted immune to the noise and motion and sat staring ahead, as if their kids were fruit flies the women would rather ignore than react to in any way. You were always that sort of woman. I was one of the children with a layer of dirt beneath my fingernails, greasy hair, clothes that always smelled of urine and cigarettes. "This place is teeming with the worst kinds of mothers," you always said, loudly enough for everyone to turn and stare.

Is you stupid? The words repeated themselves in Beth's head as she walked. Stupid. Loss is stupid. Instantly, Beth surprised herself by thinking of the new eyeglasses she'd bought the winter before. She'd saved up for them a long time; her job's health insurance didn't cover eyewear. Then, a month after she bought a smart pair of tortoise-shells, her mother sent her a new purse in the mail, an apology for some damn thing or other. She'd bought it from a sidewalk vendor;

it was the typical sidewalk vendor type of purse: cheap black vinyl onto which a designer label had been adhered with superglue.

"Tacky," Kerry had commented.

"I'm going to use it," Beth had replied. "I like its irony." She had just turned thirty-five and irony seemed valuable. She transferred her wallet and chewing gum into her new purse, forgot that her eyeglasses lived in a zippered compartment in the old purse, and threw the old bag and her glasses down the apartment building's trash chute. Presumably, it landed in the dumpster with castaway food and dirty diapers. City workers emptied the garbage early the next morning. On her way to work, Beth noticed her eyes felt tense from squinting. The loss humiliated her; she couldn't have been that stupid.

After she learned of her mother's death—as Beth walked block after block in the oppressively hot Chicago night air—she kept looking in ruts beside curbs, half expecting to see her glasses. Thirteen years ago, she'd fallen into disrepair when she'd thought her mother was dead. Would she do that again? She was thirty-five now, too old to lose everything a second time. She'd been at her job for ten years; she'd finally managed to move back to one of Chicago's more decent neighborhoods where an abundance of grocery stores stayed open all night, and maybe, soon, she would meet a woman to love.

She thought of Jersey City, where her mother lived—*had* lived, she corrected herself—where, on the worst streets, the stores sometimes closed altogether and sat abandoned for years in empty asphalt lots. If hers disintegrated into that kind of life this time, she would never again manage to climb her way back out. She sat, still not crying, on a bus stop bench in Chicago's Lincoln Park in front of a posh, twenty-four-hour market. She'd sometimes seen a homeless woman asleep in the loading dock doorway on the side of the store. She remembered one early morning when, on her way to work, she had witnessed a police officer waking this woman gently, respectfully. "Ma'am," he'd said quietly. "Ma'am you'll have to wake up now. It's morning." She remembered how, when she was small and her mother and she sometimes lived in pocket doors or parks, the police woke them with either excessive gentleness or brutality. Nothing in the middle, nothing with the indifferent manners of an alarm clock.

After walking a long time, Beth boarded a bus to downtown. Two civilian hate crime fighters—Pink Angels, they called themselves—with thick arms in pink T-shirts sat in front, near the driver. They patrolled the gay neighborhoods, making sure nobody got attacked. Beth felt as if, perhaps, she'd been looking to join them, that she should adopt a sober, fixed vigilante gaze, black jeans, a walkie-talkie—that everything would make sense in that impenetrable new life. She thought of Rachel, the only real lover she'd ever had. She'd lost Rachel the last time she'd heard that her mother had died. Her eyes stung with loneliness. At least this time there was no one other than her mother to lose. A drunk passenger across the aisle pointed up at website advertisements hanging above the bus seats, and shouted, "W.W.W. Kiss my ass dot com."

Beth laughed.

"What're you laughin' at, Olive Oyl? W.W.W Kiss my ass."

She laughed again. Her voice made a noise like a ringing telephone, filled the bus, filled the night, a cold, lonesome noise. She wanted it to stop. "Answer it," Beth told the drunk man. "Go on. Say hello."

I remember how hard it was for you to wait for our caseworker, and how waiting sometimes took all day. One afternoon, when I was nine or ten years old, we sat beside another mother and daughter. Do you remember? They both wore white straw hats and pink dresses. The girl, who was two or three at most, sat on her mother's lap, staring into her mother's eyes. For hours they sat that way; the pose broke only when one leaned toward the other to bestow a kiss on a nose or a cheek. My chest hurt worse and worse every time I heard the "mmwaaa" smack of one of their kisses or the little girl's giggle. Maybe you felt my discomfort, or maybe you merely felt your own, because you stood up in front of them and hollered, "Who's gonna read to you when you're wandering the Bardo? Just tell me that. Who's gonna read to you and me?"

Wednesday

She had taken the bus to the train and had ridden the train all night. Finally, she walked home in the early morning sun. A shirtless young man in bicycle shorts and dress shoes hobbled out of a hotel. Beth, when disintegrating after her mother's fake death, had once maintained a similar life; she'd given up her job and turned a steady trick, Kerry's father. The boy prostitute looked at Beth with something like fear or shame and wiped his nose on a bare arm. She was both pleased and ashamed to note, in his fear, that he had regarded her as superior. Perhaps she would not disintegrate again? Buses sighed past and she stopped for coffee at her usual spot, a filthy place with a poster hanging in the bathroom that read, FOUR OUT OF FIVE DOCTORS RECOMMEND HIV TESTING TO THEIR PATIENTS WHO HAVE SEX.

"You're here early." Tina, who'd worked there forever, poured coffee into a heavy paper cup. "I haven't even taken the chairs down."

"My mother died." Beth's voice seemed to echo through the coffee shop, and the phrase got stuck in the ceiling fan, where it repeated itself. *My mother died. My mother died. My mother died.* It was too early for other customers. She paid for the coffee.

It seemed that someone had switched the coffee shop door. Beth remembered having always had to push it open on her way out, but today, she had to pull. Beth didn't think those kinds of doors existed in American commerce. She thought the way out of stores was always easier, to accommodate people whose hands were full with freshly bought merchandise. Her mother had told her that when Beth was young.

At home, Kerry must have still been asleep because Sam mewed angrily in the foyer. "You need some food, Sam?" It astounded Beth how someone so "bonded" to her pet could so often forget to feed him. The kitchen floor tiles surprised her with their pale blueness. She'd always thought they were white. She hunkered down beside Sam while he ate, annoyed him with a hand on his fatty back. Outside, the day grew louder. Through the windows came the screeches of bus and car brakes, the whining clangs of dumpsters being hoisted and emptied into garbage trucks, and the miscellaneous clatter of construction machines erecting the parking garage. Amazing how much construction sites irritated her as an adult, she thought; when she and her mother were homeless, they welcomed those sites as refuges when it rained or when they wanted to piss in private.

Someone rapped on the door, and, opening it, Beth was startled to see Kerry's father, Mark. He held Kerry's hand.

"You look like shit," Mark said. She hadn't ever intended to tell him about Kerry, but she and Kerry had bumped into him and his wife, a lady doctor, at the zoo one day when Kerry was six years old. Mark had recognized himself in Kerry. "That's why you disappeared on me," he'd said.

It wasn't completely true. She hadn't known she was pregnant when she stopped coming to the hotel, but she let him believe it because it seemed an almost honorable excuse. She didn't know how he explained it to his wife, whether he'd lied and said it had been an affair, whether that would have been easier or harder for her to hear than the truth. Still, his wife had been awfully noble about it all. Mark and his doctor wife didn't give Beth any cash, but they did pay for Kerry's tuition to private schools and lessons, and they took Kerry for weekends and on trips Beth would never have been able to afford.

"Where'd you go last night? She called me at one in the morning to come get her. She was terrified."

"She's twelve," Beth said. "She's not four."

"It's not okay, Beth."

"Nothing's okay," Beth replied. Then she said, "My mother died," expecting him to soften, to understand.

"Your mother died before I ever met you." He shook his head. "It was one of the first things you ever told me. How many mothers do you have?"

"Just one."

"Right." He kissed Kerry's cheek. "Okay now, pumpkin?"

Kerry nodded.

"Okay," he said. "Be good."

Then to Beth he said, "Make sure to call me the next time your mother dies." And Beth remembered: he would always be the beguiled john and she would always be the whore. He would always have the position of power, of righteousness. She would always be just like the boy she saw outside the hotel this morning.

"I have to take you to camp right away," Beth told Kerry once Mark had gone. Kerry spent her summer days as a junior counselor for a poor kids' day camp. "What do you talk to them about?" Beth had asked Kerry once, and she'd replied, "Cats, mostly."

"I'm hungry."

But Beth knew that Kerry had eaten breakfast already. She carried the smell of syrup with her. "When I was your age, I clipped my mother's toenails, washed her hair and changed her tampons," Beth said.

"Gross. Why'd she have you do that?"

"You can eat at camp," Beth answered.

The mother you yelled at, the mother in the white straw hat, ignored you the way people often did at the AFDC. Maybe they all thought it was an act, that you could turn your craziness on and off every time your SSI came up for review. I thought that sometimes, you know. Or maybe you weren't bewitching to anyone but me. That night, you gave me a long kiss on the mouth; I tasted your cigarettes. "You'll read me through the Bardo, won't you?"

"Yes," I answered. "What's a Bardo?"

"It's limbo," you sighed as if I should have known, and as if this definition would make sense to me. "The space you have to travel between death and eternity. That's what The Tibetan Book of the Dead *is for. The living read it to the newly dead to guide them through the Bardo."*

"What book is it?" I tried hard to understand.

"Never mind." You pursed your lips and looked away. "You'd be a lousy guide anyway."

Her grandmother's heavy North Jersey accent surprised Beth a bit. Her mother had one, of course, and Beth did too once, long ago. Rachel, her last real lover, had taught her how to speak with rounded vowels. Rachel had gone to private schools and worked as an English professor; at twenty-one years old, Beth believed this qualified Rachel to do most anything.

Now, Beth sat on Kerry's unmade bed, held the telephone, tried not to notice the overwhelming feline smell coming from her daughter's sheets, and talked to her grandmother. Kerry's window overlooked the alley behind the building and pointed toward the orange cranes that threatened downtown with the promise of even more new construction. "Why didn't you call me?" she asked her grandmother. "The police said she died ten days ago. I just found out."

"You haven't called me in six years," her grandmother replied. "How was I supposed to know your number?"

"Was there anything? A memorial or anything?"

"Nah. Her boyfriend's got the ashes."

"There's got to be something."

"Don't look at me. I did all I could for her and her brother twenty-seven years ago. She's been dead to me twenty-seven years."

The quiet weight of her mother's history hung between Beth's grandmother and her. She knew that they had fought when, at sixteen years old, Beth's mother had gotten pregnant. She knew that her grandmother believed in God, divine justice, morality, and Sicilian witchcraft. Beth's grandmother alleged that her family's faith was hard won and not to be mocked. "We didn't move to America for you to get knocked up," Beth's grandmother reportedly had told her mother. It was 1972, shortly before Roe v. Wade, and Beth's mother had no money to get rid of Beth illegally, so, in 1973, Beth was born to share her mother's poverty.

When she saw Beth, though, Beth's grandmother recanted and, for eight years, tried to help. Then Jimmy died. Jimmy was Beth's mother's older brother. When he was a child, Beth's mother said, he sometimes sat in corners, banging his head into the walls. "That's where

I got it. From Jimmy," her mother had explained. Beth's mother banged her head into walls when, as she said, "things went red." But even this action didn't make it better. Nothing made it better, Beth knew, besides heroin. Jimmy turned her on to it before there was any such thing as Prozac. *But maybe heroin stopped working too,* Beth thought. *She died by blowing her brains out; it was, after all, just a fiercer way of banging her head against the wall.* Jimmy died when Beth was eight. A shop owner he was trying to rob shot him. There was an open casket memorial. She'd seen Jimmy all her life, but that was the first time she noticed that he had her mother's face.

Maybe her grandmother had also noticed their resemblance in a new and startling way. Maybe, in Jimmy's dead body, she saw the inevitability of Beth's mother's death. Or maybe she just decided she'd had enough heartbreak for one lifetime and needed distance. After Jimmy died, Beth's grandmother never spoke to her mother again. She allowed Beth to live with her, though, for two years, when Beth was nearing adolescence and her mother was temporarily institutionalized for letting something happen to Beth, something that Beth flatly refused to think about even now, decades later. When her mother got out, Beth's grandmother demanded that Beth stay with her, but Beth didn't. She went back to her mother and stayed for three years. Then she ran away for good.

"I want to do something. Some kind of memorial."

"Don't look at me."

"She was my mother. I was all she had."

"I'm the one that gave you all that money. What did she ever give you?"

"I said that I was all *she* had, not the other way around."

"I heard you," Beth's grandmother said. "But I'm talking about all that money."

By "all that money" her grandmother referred to five hundred dollars she'd loaned Beth six years earlier. Beth's mother had asked her to ask her for it. They hadn't spoken, except through Beth, since Beth was eight. "She'd let me starve if it was up to her," Beth's mother had said. Beth told her grandmother she needed the money for Kerry and gave the money to her mother. Then she stopped talking to her grandmother. She'd planned to call when she could pay her back.

I don't know much about the Bardo, you know. I haven't believed in a life after this one since I was eight years old. I believed in angels back then, remember? One night when we were sleeping in that playlot on Pavonia, I was lying on the bench and you were on the ground below me. I remember that it was late enough for the police to make us leave if they came. I leaned my hand over one side of the bench, felt gravity weighing my hand down, and told you that the weight was an angel's hand in mine. You snorted, "Why don't you just believe in God while you're dreaming?"

"Do you believe in God?" I asked you.

And you answered, "I think I saw him in a movie once."

Around that same time, I collected acorns for you: the ones that could turn into rings when rubbed against the pavement. I carried acorns in my pocket and slept with my fingers curled around them. I told myself that if I dropped them in my sleep, I would be punished and you would die.

After I heard that you'd died, I sat on a bench outside a grocery store and I saw, or imagined I guess, you and me in a field. We threw acorns at a dead tree. Yours kept shattering against the tree trunk, but my aim kept veering, landing my acorns on the ground. "What now?" you said after I'd missed the tree several times, "What now?"

I thought of how you never appreciated me, how you never saw that I was all you had. I'd always wanted to be appreciated. I'd always clung to that hope, you know, even in my sleep, just like I'd clung to those stupid acorns.

Leonard, Beth's mother's last boyfriend, was only thirty-seven years old. The police put them in contact. They'd only been dating for three months. "I loved her," he told Beth over the telephone. "But I didn't know her too well."

He couldn't have loved her, Beth decided. She asked him to say everything he knew about her. He didn't know that, when Beth was small, her mother had auburn hair to her waist that looked purple in the yellow-brown city light. He didn't know that she wore flair bottom jeans with sequined patches on the knees and a yellow shirt that read FUCK JESUS in blurry white letters you couldn't read unless you stared at them for several minutes. He didn't know that she knew the T. S. Eliot poem "Apeneck Sweeney" by heart, or that Beth knew that poem too because of her. He didn't even know that she drank grape soda. (Beth didn't remember that herself until she was talking to Leonard, and started craving it.) He didn't know that she once claimed that Rosalind Carter was the only obstacle preventing her absolute happiness, or that once, she squatted, crying, against the side of a building and said that nothing would be ever be okay unless they could bring back FDR's administration.

"Did she ever tell you about me?"

"She mentioned you."

"Why didn't you try calling me when she died?"

"I didn't know where you were. She never even told me your name. Besides, sometimes the things she said, you never knew what to believe."

"No," Beth agreed. "You never knew."

But she still felt bitter about how she'd found out. A friend's acquaintance who worked as an emergency room nurse and saw her mother's corpse had gotten the police in touch with her.

"I'm flying out there," Beth told Leonard. "We're doing something."

"We're already doing something," he replied. "All her friends. We're gonna set her ashes free at the Hudson. She loved it there."

"I should be there too."

"I don't know," he replied. "When's the last time you even saw your Ma?"

"Last Christmas." It had been Mark's turn to deal with Kerry for the holiday and it seemed a nice gesture to invite her mother to come when her mother called asking for money. It was Christmas after all. She shouldn't have had to be alone. She showed up at Beth's apartment with a boy who'd gone to high school with Beth. "Hey Ho Street," he'd said, an absurd nickname Beth had carried with her through high school. They'd driven from Jersey City in the boy's car, and they sat on Beth's couch, making out. The boy, named Jamie or Jason, Beth forgot which, had his hand up her mother's shirt. Beth's mother took off her shoes and Beth saw the holes in the toes of her nylons. She'd put them up at the Days Inn that night, because she hadn't wanted them in her house.

On her way out of Beth's apartment, her mother had raised her hands in the air. "I have checked my arms at the door," she'd said.

"Come on," Jaime/Jason had answered, his hand on her mother's elbow. "Let's just go."

Now, on the telephone, her mother's newest lover, Leonard, gave Beth directions to the Hutton Street tenement as if she'd never lived in those projects herself. Beth petted Sam until he tired of it and bit her hand away. She called Mark and told him to take care of Kerry, called her office and told Donna, her coworker, that she would be gone for two days, and then she called the airline.

It had been over one hundred degrees in Chicago, but it felt even hotter outside the Jersey City tenement, even though the air was wetter here and probably cooler. Probably, Beth decided, because the land around the crumbling brick projects offered no green whatsoever to cool the eye. No trees grew here, not even along the playlots where rusted metal jungle gyms jutted crookedly from sand. Nor was there any grass, just small plots of dirt and weeds growing through the cracks in the concrete steps that led to the small square porches at the doorways to every building. The city's lawmakers didn't notice the project anymore, didn't throw it morsels of money for repairs. The nearby businesses had bought the land and soon the homes would be razed. Many had already been vacated, their boarded windows and doors blindly, mutely facing the passing Hutton Street buses. The buildings that people still occupied looked little better than vacant themselves. Cheap aluminum doors hung askew at the tops of the cement stairs, and box fans, balanced precariously in rotting window frames, churned the heat around. Not like the Chicago projects close to where the Democratic Convention was housed; they'd received face-lifts before the public had come. "Much like the Nazis fixed Terezin up," Beth's mother would probably have said. "When visitors were due."

Her mother was fifty-one years old, Beth realized now, too old to have lived in a tenement with any degree of hope. At some point, it seemed, at some age, hope deteriorated, didn't it? At some age, the possibilities of other lives fell away and you were stuck solely with the life you were living. At some point, the only alternative route was the mouth of a gun in your mouth. She wondered if that would happen to her someday too. She wondered if it should.

"Liz?" It sounded like a sneer, an insult, and Beth turned to see the man her mother, presumably, had lived with. He looked her up and down, eyes pausing on her stomach. "You look like her," he said.

"No." Briefly, she imagined that she did look like her mother, that she was pretty enough to take the man's fingers into her mouth and lead him to bed.

"Leonard," the man reminded her.

Her body leaned toward him of its own accord and she felt a deep, secret part of herself wanting, suddenly, to conceive another baby, to leave her job, to set the life she'd built on fire again. "I don't look like her," she said aloud. Her body leaned back to its former respectable distance and Leonard's fingers held no allure at all as he gestured vaguely toward a public housing building. "I live in that one," he said. "But they're tearing them all down. Did you know?"

Beth shook her head. "Where will you go?"

"The Bronx, I guess," he said. "Everything else in this town'll get leveled soon too."

Beth couldn't imagine her mother in Leonard's tiny, immaculate apartment. The floor bore an area rug with tiger stripes. Clothes hung neatly in an open closet and a bowl of apples sat on the counter. "This isn't where your ma lived. They relocated me after," he said. "Once they made sure I wasn't the one pulled the trigger." He said that the building she'd died in would be the first of the homes to be razed. Beth wondered if anyone had cleaned her mother's brains off the wall. *It should have been my job*, she thought.

"Here's her stuff," Leonard said, drawing a cardboard box from the closet. Old clothes and dirty shoes filled the box.

"Where are her books?"

"Her books?"

"Her T. S. Eliot. Her Shakespeare."

"I never saw them."

"My mother never got rid of her books." Even when they moved from tenement to tenement, even when they lived in parks, in shelters, in bus stations, she kept them in a box, in a shopping cart. Maybe her books got too heavy for her to carry from place to place. Maybe she pared her library down to the texts she'd memorized. Maybe, Beth hoped, they reminded her of their years together too much, made her miss Beth too much. *No*, Beth thought, *Leonard didn't know her at all.*

"Ashes." Leonard brought a black urn from his bedroom. He looked ready to cry. "I like to keep her near at night."

"What did she say about me?"

"What do you mean?"

"When she mentioned me. You said she mentioned me once."

He looked at Beth, tilted his head to one side as if deciding whether to tell the truth. "She said you were a waste of time." The corners of his mouth lifted. It couldn't have been a smile, Beth decided. It must have been embarrassment, or pity, or nerves.

You wouldn't acknowledge that I was all you had. Remember how you used to say, "You ended my life." Remember how you said, "If you were a reasonable person, if there were justice in the world, you would jump off a building or run away so that I could have a chance." I remember the thick pathways of tears that dirtied your cheeks.

I never told you how, for a minute, every time you said those things, I imagined how good it might feel to have nothing but cold air above and below me, how you might look if you were happy, and I considered jumping. Then I thought about leaving you alone and knew you had no one else to take care of you. That's the thought that made me change my mind, made me say, "I'm not jumping off a building."

"Selfish," you always answered. "Narcissist."

I wanted to take care of you. That's why I waited until I was seventeen to move away. I thought you would need me and follow. I forgot how pretty you were, how easy it would be for you to find men to use you in ways that masqueraded as caring. Except when you pretended to be dead, you never even asked me to visit.

You wouldn't acknowledge I was all you had. Instead, at midnight on my birthday every year, you phoned to remind me it was the "anniversary" of your "death." Every year, you declared, "Your life contaminated the very essence of mine." But I didn't mind because I saw that I meant enough to you, that you needed me enough, to make yourself pay attention to the date and the hour, even though those kinds of details eluded you. I didn't mind. Our last conversation was just bravado, really. I'd been practicing that speech. Remember how I yelled? "How did I pollute your life? By changing your tampons for you? By doing your taxes for you?" It was only bravado. I was still angry with you about Christmas. When you hung up, I didn't know we wouldn't talk again. When you sent me the purse a month later, I took it as an apology but I didn't say thank you the way I should have. Instead, I decided to be coy and wait for more gestures. Then I lost my glasses. Five months after that, half your head was missing; you had left it behind on Leonard's living room wall. Very few women commit suicide in this way, you know. Most take pills. Some may even jump off buildings.

In the heat, Beth walked from the projects to her grandmother's. Her grandmother still lived in the rowhouse where she'd raised Beth's mother and Jimmy, where Beth herself had stayed. The neighborhood's smell was as old as Beth's memory: a quiet smell of things that had long ago been cooked. She remembered that her grandmother used to have a plastic ashtray engraved with frowning green-eyed gods beneath the word Hawaii. The ashtray sat on the living room coffee table and Beth wouldn't walk past it unless her grandmother came too. Her grandfather spoke no English but sat for hours every day in an armchair behind an open *Newark Star Ledger*. He worked as a barber and died when Beth was three years old, of a stroke. The word stroke seemed, to Beth, to belong to the same secret, dangerous, unknowable world as the Hawaii ashtray. Jimmy died five years later, and, after that funeral, after she stopped speaking to her mother altogether, Beth's grandmother got a job driving a school bus for disabled children.

Beth rang the buzzer. In her pin-striped goucho pants and white T-shirt, her grandmother looked so much smaller and less firm than she did in Beth's memories. She stood on an area rug Beth remembered from childhood; its thick colorful threads looked as if they'd been woven together on a child's plastic toy loom.

"So," she said.

On the foyer wall hung a photograph of Beth's grandmother, grandfather, and two faceless babies in white dresses. Before her grandmother did whatever she did to erase their faces, the babies had been Beth's mother and Jimmy.

"What do you want from coming?" she asked Beth. "What are you expecting to happen?"

"Commemoration, I guess. I don't know. We're doing it tonight at midnight at the river."

"You want money." It wasn't a question.

"No."

"Yeah. Yeah. You want money all right." She closed the door.

She didn't answer when Beth rang the buzzer again. Beth sat in the hallway outside her door. She realized again that her mother hadn't been raised poor. She hadn't come from a poor family. Her grandmother was working class. As an adult, now, so was Beth. Her mother's poverty was the accident, the anomaly. Her grandmother could have helped for longer than eight years, made ultimatums even. "She told me that I had the Evil Eye," her mother always said. "She turned her back on me and Jimmy."

I remember that you could climb impossibly high walls, fences, and drain-pipes. I remember that you told me at least ten different versions of Jimmy Carter's presidency, and that there were days you decided to speak only in rhyme. I remember that you believed in Jesus for two years, and briefly renamed yourself, "New Wine." I remember that you used heroin, crack, crank, speed, coke, and LSD and that you smoked sixty cigarettes a day—even during your Jesus years—but claimed that marijuana was "pedes-trian." I remember that you made crayon drawings in the corners of envelopes "to trick the post office." Sometimes the envelopes had Amy Carter's name on them, but no street address and you commanded me to mail these envelopes with their incomplete addresses and home-crafted postage.

Thursday, Midnight

Only seven men attended Beth's mother's makeshift memorial. They were all her mother's former lovers, and were of two types: drug addicts and disgruntled ex-hippies. The addicts were all around Leonard's and Beth's age. Jamie/Jason was there. "Hey, Ho Street," he answered when Beth said hello. The ex-hippies were her mother's age, smart, and full of vitriol. The younger men hugged one another, said that her mother never should have died. They didn't extend their sym-pathy to Beth. They took turns telling stories. "She took care of me," one of them said. "She knew where you could go for food boxes." He must have gotten her confused with someone else, Beth thought. Another of them talked about a white dog her mother found. She named him Coke and, although Beth had never heard about this dog, was supposedly quite attached to him. One night, the dog got lost and her mother ran through the projects shouting, "Coke! Coke!"

The ex-hippies said crueler things over the ashes. "She gave great head," one of them said, holding the urn as if making a toast. Another of his ilk responded that Nancy Reagan was rumored to share that talent, and wasn't it really too bad how Reaganomics criminalized the poor and fucked up the ghetto for everyone. *What does that have to do with my mother's death? Where's your humanity?* Beth wanted to say. Instead, she felt acutely aware of her own endangerment and watched the men circling her. They would push her down, it seemed. They would push her down and her mother's ashes would resolidify into a person who would cover Beth's screaming mouth and tear her ears in half. But it didn't happen. The men hadn't been circling her. They'd been circling the Reaganomics critic and now Leonard was beating him, and Beth was doubled over and throwing up blood into the Hudson River. Her mother would have called it "contaminating the very essence" of her life, Beth thought, but she wouldn't truly have minded. Afterward, Leonard, Jamie/Jason, and Beth went to a pub, and Beth drank coffee that had no taste at all.

They sat in the pub for two hours. The men cried, but said nothing at all to Beth. It eventually became clear to her that she was expected to pay the bill, even though she was the only one of them who hadn't ordered food or liquor. She knew she ought to have been generous because the bill wasn't expensive, but she also believed that these men didn't care about her mother; they didn't even know her. "Come on, guys," she said, "who do you think I am?" She plunked down three dollars to cover her own costs and ran. She felt nauseated, as though she were strapped to a giant, rolling wheel. She made it to the river and vomited again.

Half a month ago, I met a man on the train who'd lost his leg in a car accident. He wasn't shy about his injury, so I asked him whether it was true that residual sensation existed in missing limbs. He answered that, yes, for about two years after the accident, he felt temperature, discomfort, even itches in his missing leg more acutely than in any other part of his body. Now, he said, it was down to occasional twinges. I wonder, a year from now, if I will also be unable to apprehend the world except in terms of what I'm missing. Like you, I am alone in the fiasco of motherhood. Like you, I can climb impossibly high fences and walls. Because you couldn't, I can file my own taxes and hold a job. I chose to go to work because you didn't, but no amount of skills or experience ever gave me insight into your hurt, your insanity, or even into how you, without money or education, knew everything, it seemed, except how to love me. That insight, I realize now, was what I sought most, and I do not have any idea what I want to learn now that you're gone.

She flew back to Chicago in the morning, and, at five o'clock the next evening, retrieved Kerry from camp. Next summer, she thought, she would persuade Mark and his wife to send Kerry to a sleepover camp where girls made lanyards and talked about boys instead of cats.

"We went swimming," Kerry said. "At the Y." She pressed her fleshy, wet lips against Beth's cheek. "Did you get to go to your mom's funeral?"

Beth nodded. "Did you remember to wring out your bathing suit before you put it back in your duffel bag?"

She winced. "I'll wash it when we get home."

"Never mind. I'll do it." Now that Kerry was old enough to produce the secretions and odors of a woman, doing her laundry was a disgusting chore. Beth sighed. "I'm going out again tonight. I need time to think. You can handle being alone awhile, right?"

"Sure."

"Don't go telling your dad."

Friday

Beth didn't get home until nearly dawn, but Kerry was awake, lying in bed and kicking the wall like a toddler.

"What is it?"

Kerry's moods had never made sense to Beth. She had, after all, enough food and shelter and no real troubles. "What if you or Daddy dies like Grandma?" she asked.

"You never even met your grandmother. You shouldn't be crying about her."

Beth had only mentioned Kerry to her mother on one occasion, when Kerry was already four or five. "I made it through the whole delivery without drugs," Beth had said.

"You made it through labor without drugs?" Her mother might have even sounded impressed. "I didn't make it through *yesterday* without drugs."

"I'm not. I'm just thinking about if you or Daddy dies." Kerry sniffed thickly.

Beth sat on the edge of Kerry's bed. This is why you have children, she thought, so you still have someone to belong to after your mother dies. But she couldn't belong to Kerry. She was merely an overly tall stranger whose bills Beth was meant to pay and whose bedsheets and body and even breath smelled horrifyingly like that cat. "If one of us dies, you'll have the other one," she told Kerry.

She knew she should give Kerry some greater assurance than that. She saw, with momentary clarity, the patterns of her life as if plotted on a grid. She saw herself chasing after her mother and after surrogate mothers. She saw herself surrounded by threatening circles of men. She saw herself adopting her mother's ambivalence and blame, and infecting Kerry with them. Kerry, whom Beth was supposed to love. She saw that she should not jump off a building, that she should not disintegrate again. Instead, she was supposed to blame her mother, love her daughter, go to therapy, find a woman who loved her, maybe even more than she herself could love in return. She saw that Kerry was the key to all of it, that if she could love her daughter enough, the other patterns would vanish. She touched Kerry's arm and Kerry looked back at her, alarmed and grateful. Then the grid dissolved. She had a good job, a nice apartment, and a daughter she would never sell to a circle of men. She had surpassed her mother and, one day, Kerry would surpass Beth. "You're lucky," she told Kerry, letting go of the girl's large arm. "Look at me. I'm an orphan now."

"Poor Mommy," Kerry said. She put her heavy arms around Beth's neck. "Can I do anything for you?"

Sweet girl, Beth thought, but the acrid smell of cat overwhelmed her and the words that came were, "Just give me space."

Last night, in Chicago, a man dressed as Jesus walked behind me down Clark Street. An old woman in broken-down shoes danced on the sidewalk. A shopping cart heaped with plastic tarps, dirty clothes, and a sign that read CAR WASH stood unattended in an alley beside a pile of human feces. So many people go uncelebrated, I thought. You would have too, if it weren't for me. I'm still the only thing you have. But what I realize now is that you were all I had too. This morning, after dropping Kerry off at day camp, I bought The Tibetan Book of the Dead *and read it, but it wasn't the kind of guide you needed. So I'm giving you my own, here at the docks of Lake Michigan, so many miles from the water where your ashes float or sink, but I hope you can hear me from the Bardo if you're wandering it.*

Acknowledgements

This project was made possible through the generous funding of John and Naomi Luvass, Walter and Nancy Kidd, the University of Oregon and the University of Illinois-Chicago. It also results from the insight and constructive criticism of UIC and UO fiction-writing faculty members: David Bradley, Debra Gwartney, Ehud Havazelet, Porter Shreve, Jim Sloan, and Grace Talusan. Most of all, this project has benefited from the generous and painstaking feedback of Cris Mazza, a brilliant writer and inspirational teacher.